# IT'S HIS OTHER BABY MAMA'S FOR ME 3

## THERESA REESE

## TASHA MACK

Cole Hart
SIGNATURE NOVELS

**It's His Other Baby Mama's For Me 3**

Copyright © 2021 by Theresa Reese & Tasha Mack

All rights reserved.

Published in the United States of America.

Published by Cole Hart Signature, LLC.

**Mailing List**

**To stay up to date on new releases, plus get information on contests, sneak peeks, and more,**

*Go To The Website Below...*

**www.colehartsignature.com**

# PREVIOUSLY

In just a few short minutes, the restaurant was clear of all guests. Mir placed Remi back on the floor but made sure to hold on tight to her just in case she tried to fight Fallon again. Everybody was so focused on trying to calm Remi down that they hadn't noticed Cynthia walk through the door.

"Remi, what's going on, and why are you fighting her?" Cynthia sneered, pointing in Fallon's direction.

"Ma, I'm so sorry about this!" Remi said. The last thing she expected to be doing was fighting. She knew she was playing a dangerous game by inviting Cynthia, but she had to start somewhere. The way Remi saw it, if they were in a public place, Cynthia would react better. It had taken months for Remi to get Cynthia to agree to coming to the event. She also had to lie and tell her that Ryleigh wouldn't be there. Remi turned around and looked at Ryleigh with a pleading look in her eyes.

All eyes were on Ryleigh as she came face to face with her mother for the first time since she was thirteen years old. The last time she saw her mother, she was being handcuffed and placed into the back of a squad car.

"Remi, is this some sort of joke?" Cynthia asked as she looked back and forth between Ryleigh and Fallon.

"Ma, I can explain everything. I know you told me that you don't want to have anything to do with Ryleigh, and I know that you're still hurting about how everything went down, but that's still your daughter!" Remi explained. Overcome with emotion, Ryleigh could no longer hold back the tears in her eyes. Unsure of what was going on, Zay instinctively wrapped his arms around Ryleigh to console her.

"You damn right I don't want to have shit to do with that little lying ass bitch!" Cynthia spat with venom lacing her voice. She hated Ryleigh, and nothing would ever change the way she felt.

"Liar? Did you ever once try to ask me what happened?" Ryleigh quizzed, stepping away from Zay.

"I don't have to ask you anything! I know exactly what happened, you little jealous bitch!"

"You still the same ol' snooty ass bitch from back in the day." Fallon smirked as she walked up on Cynthia. Isa and Ryleigh looked at each other in confusion.

"Well, if it isn't Ms. Side Bitch herself," Cynthia shot back.

"Ma, what are you talking about?" Remi asked, furrowing her brows together.

"That's right, and I was a damn good one at that! You always hated how Isaac made sure that Isa was well taken care of. What you thought, he was going to get me pregnant and then leave me hanging?" Fallon said, using the napkin to wipe blood from her swollen lip.

"He treated you like the cum bucket you are! You think I wasn't home the day you dropped her off on my doorstep? Yeah, I was there, but don't ever think for a second I was giving any of my husband's insurance money to that bastard of a child!" Cynthia revealed.

"Hold on. What the hell is going on?" Isa spoke up. She was getting tired of them talking in circles, she needed answers.

"This is the bitch who kept you from your father for all those years before he died," Fallon replied, causing everyone to gasp. Shocked, Ryleigh walked in Fallon's direction.

"That day at the mall, you knew who we were, didn't you?" Ryleigh asked.

"How could I not? You look just like that nigga Isaac," Fallon snapped.

"So, Ryleigh and Remi are my sisters?" Isa asked in disbelief. Fallon nodded her head yes, never taking her gaze off Cynthia. She felt like it was Cynthia's fault for the way she had to raise her daughter.

"Are you fucking serious? So, run that shit by me again?" Zay tried to piece everything together.

"Ma, is this true?" Remi asked Cynthia for clarity.

"This isn't about Fallon's bastard child. This has everything to do with Ryleigh and what she did!"

"What I did? You don't even know what happened!" Ryleigh cried as she faced her mother. It had been almost nine years and Cynthia showed that she didn't give a damn about Ryleigh by not accepting any of her phone calls, responding to any letters, or coming to any visits.

"I know exactly what happened! They must not know you for the conniving, jealous bitch you really are. I'm sure if they knew the real you, they wouldn't feel the same. Go ahead and tell your sister what you did," Cynthia spat.

"Why are you doing this? Do you hate me that much?" Ryleigh cried as Zay grabbed her hand.

"Go ahead and tell Fallon and her bastard child what you did to their precious Isaac. Tell them how you murdered your father in cold blood, Ryleigh!" Cynthia revealed.

☙  I  ❧

All eyes were on Ryleigh as she nervously shifted her weight to her left leg as she tried her best to mentally process all of the events that had led up to that very moment. Every feeling that she had been suppressing was now threatening to rear its ugly head. She looked at Cynthia, the woman who gave her life, and saw nothing but hate in her eyes. Remi, who was standing next to Cynthia, gave her a pleading look as if to say, *I'm sorry.* Isa, her newfound sister who she had inadvertently grown close to over the last few months, wore a look of hurt mixed with confusion.

Then there was Zay, the man who unofficially held her heart, whose face held no emotion. In fact, his eyes had turned dark and it was almost like Ryleigh could see into the depths of his soul. There was a strong possibility that Cynthia's revelation would be detrimental to her relationship with Zay, but that was something she'd have to deal with later. Ryleigh had to focus on what was happening at that very moment. What explanation would she offer? Would they understand? Her breathing became rapid as visions of that horrible night invaded her thoughts. Never in a million years did she think she'd be faced with this scenario. She had worked so hard to push that horrifying night

THERESA REESE & TASHA MACK

into the back of her mind. No, she didn't want to go through that. Not here. Now just wasn't the time. Remi didn't waste any time rushing over to her sister's side. She felt bad because none of this would be happening if she would've never invited their mother in the first place.

"Go ahead and tell them, Ryleigh!" Cynthia reiterated, with an amused smirk on her face.

Ryleigh wiped her clammy hands on the front of her dress. The golf-sized lump that had formed in her throat made her feel like she was suffocating. With tears streaming down her face, she shook her head from left to right. No matter how bad she wanted Cynthia to acknowledge the truth, she knew that she wouldn't.

"I-I can't," Ryleigh finally said. Zay glanced at her once more, his jaw muscles flexed, a clear indication of his anger. He never once thought to look into the reason why Ryleigh had spent all those years in prison. In his eyes, she was such a genuine person that he felt like he didn't have to. Ryleigh could tell that he, too, wanted an answer, and when she didn't offer one, he simply walked away. For the second time in her young life, it felt like her heart had fallen into the pit of her stomach. Suddenly, she felt sick. Remi held on tight to her to keep her from falling while gently rubbing her back.

"So, wait, you killed my father?" Isa's lip twisted up in a scowl. The rage in her eyes was evident. She was stunned. Her whole life, she longed for her father to save her. She knew he was dead, but hearing that her newfound sister was the reason fucked her up. At that moment, she started questioning if she could still be cool with Ryleigh.

"Our father, Isa," Ryleigh mumbled, looking into Isa's face. Isa chuckled and shook her head.

"But why, Ryleigh?" Isa searched Ryleigh's face for an answer, when she didn't give her one, Isa walked over to the bar to grab her clutch before leaving the restaurant. Zane was hot on her heels talking to her, but Isa tuned everything out around her. In one swift motion, he grabbed her from behind. Zane wrapped his strong arms around her tiny waist.

"Ma, c'mon, stop, talk to me, yo," he whispered into her ear. Isa's breath was caught in her chest. "Don't run, please." Isa was tired of running but at this point, she didn't know what to do. Isa held her chest, heaving heavily.

"How? Like, how?" she cried. Zane turned her around and rocked from side to side with her face buried in his chest.

"Isa, how the hell you storm out like that?" Fallon shouted as her heels clicked across the concrete. "I haven't seen you in God knows how long and I walk into bullshit."

"If you come any closer, I'ma lay your conniving ass out clean," Zane spoke through clenched teeth. "Get the fuck from 'round here."

Fallon laughed in his face. "I'm not going a damn place, you may scare other people but you damn sure don't scare me."

"Bitch." Zane let Isa go, but Isa stepped forward.

"Zane, she's not even worth it." She turned to Fallon, squinting her eyes. "You knew they were my sisters and you hid that shit from me. Not only have you been selling me to the highest bidder, you've been having me alone and I had two sisters out here."

"They don't give a damn about you and you're too stupid to see that shit. You saw the way their mother talked about you." Fallon squeezed the bridge of her nose. "She called you a bastard child!"

"It's not about them, it's about you!" Isa shouted, breaking free of Zane. She stepped in her mother's direction. "On everything I love, which isn't much, you better not ever cross paths with me or the next time that will be ya ass!" Isa turned on her heels, coming face to face with Tayvin. She squinted her eyes and furrowed her brows.

"You that little bitch I drove to the hospital a few years back, ain't it?" Tayvin licked her lips. "This the bitch you fucking with, Zane? A whole hoe?"

"Tayvin, take your certified ass home. Where the fuck is my son?" He walked up on her, but Isa grabbed a hold of his arm. By now, everyone was out of the restaurant standing on the corner. "Your son is with 'our' girlfriend." She rolled her neck for emphasis.

"Yeah, see Zane, I'm not doing this shit." Isa threw up her arms. "You can have her and that other bitch, and Ma, take heed to what the fuck I said." Isa heard Tayvin arguing with Zane. All she kept repeating was how Isa was a hoe and he was stupid for leaving his family. She flagged down a cab and got in before Zane could catch up to her.

"I can't believe this shit," she mumbled before rambling off the address to the apartment to get her car. Isa wanted to be long gone before Zane showed up.

4

## ❧ 2 ☙

Zay had heard enough. The fact that Ryleigh didn't offer an explanation as to why she'd killed her father told him everything he needed to know. Had he known that, he would've never pursued her. His father had died at the hands of his mother, and he hated her for that. He noticed everything about Ryleigh, so how could he have missed that? Hopping in his car, Zay pulled out a blunt from the center console. He lit it and took a long pull. The ringing of his phone jarred him from his thoughts.

When Zay saw Ryleigh's name flash across the screen, he powered his phone off. He didn't want to talk to her and the way he was feeling, he wasn't sure if he ever would. Zay had made it clear to Ryleigh on more than one occasion how he felt about his mother and what she did and still, she chose not to tell him she had killed her father.

Right now, his main focus was to make sure the operations of the restaurant ran smoothly. This was not what he had pictured for his grand opening. They had spent months making sure a plan was devised to bring in as much revenue as possible. Since he was well connected, Zay was sure the grand opening would be the talk of the town. One minute he was making his rounds, ensuring that everyone was having a good time, and the next, all hell had broken loose. Just like everyone else, he was shocked when Cynthia walked in. Nothing in the world could have prepared him for the words that came out of her mouth.

Twenty minutes later, he was using his key to enter Jasmine's apartment. He looked around at her well-kept living space. He wasn't sure why he was there, but he remembered at one point in time, Jasmine's company used to bring him peace of mind. They weren't on the best of terms, but he wanted them to be cordial for the sake of co-parenting.

"Zay? What are you doing here?" Jasmine asked as she dried her hair with a towel. She was fresh out the shower with a terry cloth towel wrapped around her petite frame. Her almost nine-month-pregnant belly was protruding, giving him an open view of her freshly waxed pussy.

"This my shit, I can come up in this mufucka whenever I feel like it." He shot back as he sat down on the couch. Jasmine knew Zay better than he knew himself. He appeared cool and level headed on the outside, but she knew better. Something was bothering him.

"Trouble in paradise?" she asked as she went to the kitchen and grabbed his favorite drink. She wasn't much of a drinker, but she always kept a house full of liquor for Zay. She pulled out a small glass from the cabinet and filled it halfway with Hennessy. She returned and handed him the glass with a sexy smile on her face.

"Nah, ain't shit goin' on, shorty," Zay answered. Zay was far from stupid, he knew what Jasmine was doing. He may have been mad at Ryleigh, but he would never let her know that. Speaking bad on Ryleigh was something that he would never do. The last time he talked to Jasmine, she threatened to tell Ryleigh about her and the baby.

Jasmine knew he was lying, but who was she to question him? Here he was, in the flesh, sitting on her couch after he'd told her that he didn't want to have anything to do with her. Jasmine was fully aware of the fact that Zay was in love with Ryleigh, but the bulge in his pants said otherwise. If he was there, it was simply because he wanted to be. By the time she was done, Jasmine wanted to make sure Ryleigh was a distant memory. Once she was out of the picture, she and Zay could be happy and raise their child in the same household.

She couldn't deny the fact that Zay was sexy as hell in his black Givenchy suit, and his Gucci cologne made her pussy wet. She waited until he was finished drinking the whole glass of Hennessy before she sprang into action.

Licking her plump lips, she tugged at his pants. Like she knew he would, Zay stood up and unbuckled his pants. Jasmine was now face to face with Zay's semi-erect dick. Her mouth watered as she stroked him and watched the size of it grow. He grabbed a handful of her wet hair as she firmly wrapped her lips around his dick.

The only thing that could be heard was slurping and moaning as Jasmine deep throated him. Once he felt his nut building up, he pumped in and out of her mouth vigorously, causing her to gag. Once he had released all his seeds down her throat, he went to the linen closet and grabbed a towel so he could clean himself up. Zay walked back into the living room to a naked Jasmine. Her legs were spread wide like she was expecting him to return the favor. When she noticed that he was heading towards the door, she hopped up with a quickness.

"Where do you think you're going?" Jasmine asked with her hands resting on her swollen belly.

"I got some shit I need to take care of," Zay answered as he grabbed his keys and exited her apartment. Zay meant what he said. He would never again stick his dick in Jasmine, but that didn't mean she couldn't top him off.


Between blowing up Zay's line and Isa's line, Zane was mentally drained. Not only was he pissed at the scene that unfolded at his grand opening, he was vexed that Isa pulled another disappearing act. He knew their brand-new relationship wasn't perfect, but he figured they were past the childish bullshit. With no place to go, he feared Isa would get caught up with Fallon again. Zane sat at the bar downing another shot of Patrón when his phone alerted him of an incoming text. He placed the glass down on the countertop, sighing heavily. When he saw "*Lil' baby*" plastered on the screen, he nearly dropped the phone trying to unlock it.

**Lil' baby: Zane, don't be mad at me but I can't continue to do this. For once in my life, shit was going well, and now I'm hit with more unnecessary drama and secrets, and to top it off, your baby mama is not someone I want to deal with. Thank you for trying to be with me but what I'm looking for you just can't give me. We both are damaged and have baggage. I am safe though, so don't trip.**

Zane furrowed his brows in confusion. He didn't even bother to text her back. He wasn't the one for the phone tag. "The fuck she mean, thank you?" He hopped to his feet. "This girl gonna make me gray before I turn twenty-three." Zane grabbed up his keys and rushed out the apartment. When he stepped out of the building, Tayvin was standing there with a small knife in her hands and a wicked smile on her face.

"Bitch, you better get the fuck away from my car!"

"I'm not going anywhere, so you better calm down before I make a scene on your block." Tayvin had always been vindictive, and now he regretted getting in too deep with her. Not only was she withholding his son from him and trying her best to stay in business with him, but her popping up to the restaurant and approaching Isa was where he drew the line.

"Tayvin, I'm not playing with your sick ass. I will literally take off my belt and whoop ya ass like a bad-behaved kid." Zane stepped forward in her direction, causing Tayvin to hop around the car and out of his reach. Zane stopped and breathed heavily before taking another step towards her. Tayvin wasn't looking and lost her footing. She tripped on the high curb and came crashing down. Zane grabbed her to her feet, dangling her in the air. "Keep fucking with me, you nutty bitch, and I'm going to get your ass admitted to the nearest nut house." The fear in her eyes showed she had come back down to reality. Zane knew she was off her meds, but he had no intentions of keeping tabs on her schedule. He had given her four years of his life and their course had run out.

"I'm sorry, Zane," Tayvin whispered, pulling Zane back to the situation. Lowering her down to the ground, he dropped her hard on the concrete.

"If I catch you back over here and it's not to drop off my son, I'm going to fuck you up, do you hear me?" Zane asked in a chastising voice.

Tayvin shook her head fast. Jumping to her feet, she scurried to her parked car. At one point in his life he thought Tayvin was the best thing that had happened to him. She was older, smart, and beautiful. Her saving him that day outside only made him follow her around like a lost puppy. His brothers always warned him that something was off with her, but Zane was pussy whipped and love stricken. It wasn't until one day when their son was born that he learned she was bipolar. He should have walked away with his infant son, but he didn't know if he could raise a baby alone. Zane leaned up against the car thinking about how he found his son that night.

*Zane rushed through the door after midnight with one thing on his mind, making sure his family was safe. When he stepped foot in the dark apartment, an eerie feeling came over him. He expected Tayvin to be up feeding his son on the recliner like any other night but instead, it was quiet. Zane retreated to the bedroom where their son's crib was and it was empty.*

*"Tayvin," he called out. She didn't answer and she wasn't in the bed. Zane went to leave the room when he heard the faint cries from his son. He turned on his heels and headed to where the cries were coming from. He opened the closet and found Zion in the laundry basket with a sheet on top of him. Instantly picking him up and soothing him, Zion checked to make sure he didn't have any marks on him. When he saw that he was fine, Zane went to the only other room in the house, the bathroom. Tayvin was sitting in the tub rocking back and forth with black mascara running down her face. Zane stared at her for a few minutes before speaking.*

*"What the fuck happened, Tayvin?" His voice was stern.*

*"I, I, umm, Zane, I can't, I can't be a mommy." Tayvin broke out in tears. "I don't deserve him, I don't deserve you." She was talking in riddles, which only upset Zane.*

*"Say what the fuck you gotta say, Tayvin." Zane marched back and forth, bouncing Zion on his chest. "You put my son in a laundry basket? What type of shit you on?"*

*"You don't want me, you just love him. Ever since he's come home, you don't love me anymore and I can't love him like you, just let me go, please." Zane's heart fluttered when she spoke. Yeah, he had been back running the streets only two weeks after the birth of their son, but with Tayvin not working he had to step up and get money.*

*"Don't talk like that, ma." Zane dropped to his knees and placed Tayvin's head on his shoulder. "I ain't going nowhere, I got you just like you got me."*

*"You promise?" she asked in almost a whisper.*

*"I promise."*

*"Zane, I'm bipolar and before I do anything to hurt my son, I'll leave him." She closed her eyes. "I should have told you but I've been on my medicine, and with the new baby schedule I haven't remembered to take them."*

*"Shh, we gonna fight this shit, ma. I'm making a schedule, aight."*

*"I love you," she cooed. In that moment, Zane was happy and at peace knowing she opened up to him.*

*"I love you too, ma."*

The sound of a screeching car pulled him from his thoughts. He tried to stick it out, but it only made Tayvin dependent on his presence, and when he didn't give her her way, she stopped taking her meds and started acting out. Zane hit the top of his car before hopping in the driver's seat. Isa had him worried, Casey was acting ditzy, and Tayvin was on some catch-back shit. If he needed a reason to take a vacation, now was the time. Zane drove to JFK airport. In his car, he booked a flight to Miami. A few days away was what he needed to get his mind right. He shot a text to his brothers and parked his car in the parking lot of the airport.

In the airport, Zane sat on the chair, powering his phone off and zoning out until his flight boarded.

S adness was the only word to describe how Ryleigh felt. It had been two days since the grand opening and all she had been doing was drowning in her sorrows. Here she was, four months pregnant and nobody knew but her and Zay. How could he be so cruel? Why didn't he allow time for her to explain? Furthermore, how could he just leave her during her most vulnerable time? At this point, Ryleigh had way more questions than she did answers.

Ryleigh tried her best to understand why Remi thought inviting their mother to the grand opening was a good idea. She knew Remi meant no harm, and Ryleigh had tried to get her to understand that their mother hated her. Nothing would ever change that. Ryleigh had to force herself to understand that. Was it ideal? No, but she couldn't go back in time and change the way things happened.

Then there was Isa. All her life she had been longing for her father, only for Fallon to sell her to the highest bidder. For days, Ryleigh had been consumed with guilt. If it wasn't for her, Isa would have gotten a chance to know him. She was sure Isa hated her, hence the reason she refused to answer any of Ryleigh's calls. Within minutes, her life had transitioned. She went from being close friends with Isa to finding out that they were in fact sisters. Truth be told, Ryleigh had felt a close connection to Isa the moment she laid eyes on her. She now understood why they were so much alike.

It was nine in the morning and Ryleigh finally got out the bed and showered. Her body was sore and aching from lying in the bed for so long, but the hot water from the shower provided her with some form of relief. Once she was finished oiling her body down with her favorite shea butter, she pulled out her laptop and began looking for apartments. She had saved up a nice amount of money from working at Top Notch, and Zay's weekly deposits only added to that.

There was no way in hell she was staying at Remi's with a baby. She loved her sister and knew she would be a great aunt, but she needed her own space. Everything had been happening so fast, and the initial shock of finding out that she was with child still hadn't worn off.

"You're looking for apartments," Remi stated, scaring her half to death. She came in and sat down on Ryleigh's bed, folding her legs Indian style.

"I mean, I can't live here with you forever."

"I know that, Ry, but does it have to be so soon? I know you're probably mad at me, but don't move. I guess I'm still kind of getting used to the fact that you're really home now," Remi pleaded as a look of sadness flashed across her face. Ryleigh got up from her desk and sat down next to Remi and rested her head on her shoulder. All their lives it had been just the two of them, and now that they knew that Isa was their sister, she wanted to include her too.

"It won't be so bad, Rem, just think, now that we know Isa is our sister, we can all spend more time together," Ryleigh suggested.

"That sounds good, but she hasn't even answered the phone for us, Ryleigh. And when she does, we need to meet up with her so we can sit down and talk. You need to tell her what happened that night, Ryleigh," Remi said, giving her a stern look. Ryleigh's eyes started to water at just the mere thought of reliving such a painful night. She didn't want to go there, she was still too fragile.

"I can't," Ryleigh said, just above a whisper.

"You can! And you will! You *owe* her an explanation. He was her father too. Don't worry, I'll be with you the entire time, boo."

"You tell her."

"No, she needs to hear it from you," Remi replied with finality. "Just give her a few more days to process her thoughts. She'll reach out."

"But what if she hates me?"

"Listen, this is going to be hard for us all, but we'll get through this together," Remi said, hugging her sister. "Now, back to this moving situation, why so sudden?"

"I just want my own space, that's all," Ryleigh half lied. Originally, she and Zay had planned to announce the pregnancy together but like Isa, he was upset so he refused to answer any of her calls.

"No, seriously Ryleigh? How do you just need your own space and I'm never here?" Remi quizzed, giving her the side eye.

"Okay, maybe that's not all. So, a few days before the grand opening, I found out I was pregnant," Ryleigh revealed. She fully expected Remi to go off on her for getting pregnant, but she didn't. Instead, she jumped up and pulled Ryleigh off the bed so she could examine her.

"Are you serious? Oh my gosh, I'm going to be an auntie?" Remi squealed in delight. "How far along are you?"

"Four months."

"Ryleigh, you've been hiding a pregnancy for four whole months? Why didn't you tell me?" Remi asked with a hurt expression on her face.

"Did you hear anything I said? I just told you, I found out a few days before the grand opening, crazy," Ryleigh repeated.

"Oh okay, my bad. I hope it's a girl. We're gonna take pictures in matching outfits and get our nails and stuff done," Remi rambled.

"Remi, you hardly ever go get your nails done." Ryleigh laughed. "Where is Mir? I'm about to call his ass and tell him to come and get you."

"Girl, all about my niece, we'll go and get our shit done every week. I just got off the phone with Mir. He said he was pulling up at the prison to go see his mom," Remi explained. "Anyway, I'm about to do some online shopping for the baby! Zay better get his shit together, I would hate to have to pull up on his ass," Remi threatened as she exited the room. Ryleigh couldn't do nothing but chuckle at her sister. Remi was small but every bit of rowdy when she needed to be. The way she handed Fallon's ass to her only proved that. Now that she knew about the pregnancy, it was like she had completely forgotten about Ryleigh wanting to move into her own place. Her focus was now on shopping for the new addition.

Ryleigh sat back down with her laptop to continue her search. Stumbling across a two-bedroom apartment in Manhattan, she sent the landlord a message letting her know that she was interested. She was surprised when the landlord hit her back up instantly, asking if she could come and view the condo within the next two hours. Ryleigh couldn't help the grin that quickly spread across her face. For the first time in life, she was doing something major on her own, and it felt good.

An hour later, Ryleigh pulled up in front of the complex that she soon hoped to call home. After tipping her Uber driver, she stepped out of the car looking better than she actually felt. If she didn't learn anything else from Cynthia, it was to always look your best. She had been rocking a bun at the top of her head ever since the fight with Leah, but that only accentuated her beauty. Taking the elevator up to the third floor, she walked down the long hallway as she inhaled the scent of fresh paint. She was a few minutes early, so she hoped that the landlord didn't mind. If she was too early, she fully intended to stand outside and wait.

A few seconds later, she knocked on the door. After waiting for what seemed like forever, the door finally swung open. The lady that opened the door looked like she had come fresh off of a runway. She was nothing short of gorgeous. Taken aback by her beauty, Ryleigh offered her a smile. The young woman who stood before her looked like money, and that, she couldn't compete with. Not that she didn't have her own money, she just wasn't clocking any major figures. So, if Miss Runway Model had more money to offer the land lady than Ryleigh, the apartment was as good as gone.

"Hi, I was looking for the land lady, I'm a few minutes early but she's supposed to be showing me this apartment," Ryleigh informed. The lady, who was dressed in an all-white business casual suit and red-bottom heels, glanced at her Rolex before looking back up at Ryleigh.

"I'm sorry, you must be Ryleigh. I wasn't expecting you for another twenty minutes or so, but please do come in!" she offered, stepping to the side allowing Ryleigh room to come in. She imagined the landlord to be an elderly lady, not the stunning dark-skin beauty in front of her. She scanned the vacant apartment in awe as she visualized the different ways she could decorate her future home. Relieved, she took a deep breath and walked into the luxurious living space.

"I'm Dior, by the way. Trust me, girl, you're gonna love this place." Dior smiled.

"Oh wow, it's so spacious in here," Ryleigh noted as she took in the open living room and kitchen concept. She walked into the kitchen and ran her hands across the smooth granite counter top. The appliances were stainless steel, which only added to the elegant space. She knew she would have to get Remi over to cook on the six-range stove, because if she dare tried to cook she would probably burn the whole building down.

"Aight, I'm outta here. Hit me up later, shorty," a familiar voice said coming out of the bathroom, causing Ryleigh to whip her head around in his direction.

"I'm sorry, this is a client of mine and he was just leaving."

"Mir?" she couldn't believe her eyes. She watched intently as Mir finished buttoning up his shirt. Something definitely didn't add up about the situation, because Mir told Remi that he was going to visit his mother at the women's prison in Virginia. Unless his mother had been miraculously released, she had reason to think Mir was stepping out on her sister. Why else would he lie? Mir didn't offer an explanation when he glanced in Ryleigh's direction.

"Sup Ryleigh, I'll holla at you later, Dior," he replied as he headed towards the door. Dior furrowed her brows together in confusion as she waited for Mir to walk out of the door.

"You two know each other?" Dior quizzed. Ryleigh's attitude was now written all over her face, but she had to remind herself that she didn't know the situation; therefore, it wasn't a good idea to jump to conclusions. She wanted to scream, "Yeah, bitch, that's my sister's man!"

Instead, she said, "Oh, I used to go to school with him," Ryleigh lied, in hopes that Dior would give her more detail about Mir being her so-called *client*. "So, he was looking to rent this apartment?" Ryleigh asked when she didn't say anything else.

"Oh no, Zamir is looking to invest in another property that I'm selling and he met me here to go over some last-minute details," she explained as her heels click clacked against the tile.

"I see," Ryleigh noted.

"It looks like you're pretty fond of the kitchen, let's do a grand tour, shall we?" Dior smiled as she showed her around the apartment.

Isa watched her phone ring for the fifth time in a row. She wanted to toss the phone out the window, but she knew she was only going to regret it later. Silencing yet another incoming call, Isa pulled herself up from the comfortable mattress. Isa had checked into her new favorite hotel, SIXTY Soho, a few days ago, and the stay was well needed. With her funds running low, she had to make a decision on her next move. Using her spare time, she booked her flight to Virginia for classes, which were starting in two weeks. Isa contemplated leaving over and over until it made sense. She had nothing else up here to be grateful for. Her mother was a pimp, her father was killed, her newfound sisters were a mess within itself, and Zane was just too much to handle. Without a job and a place to stay, Isa was forced to get away. Sitting up in the bed, she looked around the room. Her clothes and shoes were thrown around the room, causing her to twist up her lip in disgust. Isa wasn't a messy chick but after the last few days, she didn't have the energy nor brain capacity to do anything other than handle her hygiene. When she hopped out of the bed, her phone rang yet again. Throwing a tantrum, she saw Ryleigh's name pop up on the screen. She rolled her eyes in frustration. She and Ryleigh had grown so close, Isa had basically told her and Remi her whole life story, so for Ryleigh to not even open up about her dark past had Isa vexed. Not to mention, she was the reason Isa had grown up with the life she had. Could she fault Ryleigh? She was unsure. What she was sure of was that Ryleigh gave her no explanation when she asked. Isa silenced the call and sent her a text.

**Isa: Yeah? Wassup?**

She placed her phone back in the bed and went to start gathering her belongings. Her checkout day was in two days. She had to mentally prepare herself to either face Ryleigh or Zane, and at this moment, it was fuck both of them. The vibration on her watch startled her as she carried the clothes. In the midst of grabbing items, the call picked up.

"Yo, Isa, on the real, you need to grow up and face me like a woman."

"Zane, if you have forgotten, I'm only eighteen, so save the I'ma strong black woman speech for one of your baby mamas."

"Fuck all that you saying, 'cus I ain't hearing it. The only thing I'm hearing is I'm not woman enough to handle what life throws my way." Isa dropped the items from her hands and sprinted to the bed. She picked up her phone to continue the call.

"Nigga, are you out of your mind? I'm not this stupid, gullible ass bitch that you think I am. Yes, I fucked up by thinking you were the one, but obviously, one too many baby mamas woke me the fuck up." Isa had to catch her breath. "When I said I was done, Zane, I meant it in a nice way, but you can't take a hint so let me be clear: fuck you and everything you stand for!" Isa hung up before Zane could reel her back in. Pissed that she allowed him to bring her out of character, Isa went and blocked his number. She noticed Ryleigh had responded to her message.

**Ry: Isa, we need to talk, can we link up?**

Isa wanted to curse her out as well, but something told her to not count her out completely just yet.

**Isa: Obviously I don't have a choice with the way you and your sister have been blowing me up, so fine.**

Isa knew the last message would leave a sour taste in Ryleigh's mouth but at this point, she didn't give a damn about how bitchy she was acting, anyone could feel her wrath.

. . .

**Ry: I'ma let that slide because you're mad, but you can lose the attitude, Isa, fa'real.**

**Isa: Lose the attitude? Do you care that my life was shifted and set in stone because of you and I couldn't even get an explanation as to why?**

Isa was typing so fast as the tears fell from her eyes onto the iPhone screen.

**Isa: Forget it, just send me where you want to meet and time.**

Isa took a deep breath and waited on Ryleigh to give her a time and place. When she told her later on in the evening, Isa searched through her clothes for an outfit and then packed up her belongings. She thought if her sisters wanted to talk then cool, they could talk, and she would be bringing up that she needed a place to stay—that was until next week when she decided to go off to college and leave everyone behind. It was time for Isa to manipulate any situation to her advantage.

# ❧ 4 ❧

Once Dior finished giving her a tour of the apartment, Ryleigh informed her that she would contact her the following day to let her know if she wanted to proceed. She wanted to talk to Remi first to tell her what had happened with Mir. Delivering bad news was not something she'd planned on doing. Ryleigh thought Mir was better than that, but obviously she was wrong. He was no different than his brothers. She was also irritated by Isa's flip ass mouth, and if the situation were under different circumstances she would've cursed her out. Instead, she had to take it for what it was and accept the ridicule that came behind what she had done.

The smell of meatloaf greeted her nostrils as she opened the front door. Ryleigh sat her purse down on the kitchen table and sighed heavily. She watched as Remi moved around the kitchen, and she hated to be the one to put her sister in a bad mood, but she had to tell her.

"Hey, sister, I didn't hear you come in. I cooked your favorite." Remi smiled as she took the meatloaf out the oven. "Did you like the apartment?"

"Remi, I need to tell you something." Ryleigh hesitated when she heard a knock on the door. Swinging the door open, she stared into the scowling face of Isa. Without speaking, Isa brushed past her and walked into the living room and stood there with her arms folded across her chest. Ryleigh wanted to check her about her little attitude but decided against it once Remi came into the living room.

"Oh, y'all didn't tell me we were having this talk tonight," Remi said, looking back and forth between Ryleigh and Isa. The tension in the room was thick, and Ryleigh's stomach felt like it was in knots. If she wasn't pregnant, she would have a drink to calm her nerves.

"Let's just cut straight to the chase. Ryleigh, I need to know why you felt the need to kill my fucking father!" Isa spat.

"Who the fuck are you talking to?" Ryleigh shot back, stepping closer to Isa.

"Hold on, let's back up. I know you're upset, trust me, I get it. But what we not gon' do is be hostile towards each other. We are all sisters and we need to stick together. Both of y'all sit down so we can talk. Isa, you need to calm down and give her a chance to explain, and Ryleigh, you're pregnant and I don't need you stressing the baby!" Remi spoke in an authoritative tone. Ryleigh rolled her eyes upward. She felt where Remi was coming from, but Isa had one more time to talk crazy to her before she snapped. Isa finally sat down on the couch and gave Ryleigh her undivided attention. Ryleigh's heart started beating rapidly as she did her best to control her breathing. She didn't want to relive the past, but she owed it to her sister to tell her the truth. Hopefully, Isa caught every word, because Ryleigh vowed that this was the last time she would ever speak on the night she killed her father.

"Let me just start off by saying that this is not easy for me. I've had to live with this for the last nine years, and as much as I wish

I could take it back, I can't." Ryleigh sat down next to Isa and looked at her long and hard. She never noticed before, but Isa had their father's eyes. Taking a deep breath, she continued. Remi sat on the arm of the couch and rubbed Ryleigh's back as the tears began to freely flow.

"Growing up, Rico gave us everything we asked for," Ryleigh started.

"Wait, why are you referring to him as Rico?" Isa asked with a perplexed look on her face.

"I'm not sure why Fallon never told you, but our father's first name is Rico but he went by Isaac, which is his middle name," Remi added.

"Anyway, Daddy gave us everything growing up. Nothing was ever off limits to his girls," Ryleigh reminisced.

*It was a hot summer day and Remi and Ryleigh were outside jump roping and eating popsicles when Isaac came outside with the biggest smile on his face. He had a surprise for his family. He had put in the work to make sure his girls were comfortable, and now he wanted them all to enjoy the fruits of his labor.*

*"Hey, Daddy, look what I can do," Ryleigh called out as she held her popsicle between her teeth while she showed him how long she could jump rope without messing up.*

*"That's nice, baby girl. You did a great job. You and Remi, come in the house. I gotta surprise for y'all," he said. Once they were in the house, Cynthia came out of the kitchen eager to hear what her husband had to say.*

*"Alright, so y'all know Daddy been working a lot lately, right. I know space has been tight, so guess what?"*

*"What is it, baby?" Cynthia asked impatiently.*

*"I bought us a three-bedroom house!" he revealed. Both Remi and Ryleigh jumped up and down as Cynthia fell into his arms and kissed him passionately. They had lived in the projects all of their lives, and now it was time to move on to bigger and better things.*

*"So, does that mean we get our own room? I don't wanna share rooms with Ryleigh anymore because she snores too loud!" a seven-year-old Remi complained.*

*"Yes, princess, you both get your own rooms," Isaac confirmed.*

"I remember that! We argued over who was going to get the biggest room and, of course, I did, because I'm the oldest." Remi smiled as she recalled how happy they were the day they moved into their new home. Isa rolled her eyes upward.

"Y'all can save the happy memories. Let's not forget while y'all were living it up, me and my mother were in Jersey struggling," Isa spat.

"You think I give a fuck about you and Fallon struggling? Do you know the day we moved in that house my whole life changed forever? Cynthia started working the night shift at the hospital because it paid more. From that very first night, Isaac would come in my room and touch on me!" Ryleigh cried. "He did things a grown ass man should've never done to his daughter! This shit happened every fucking night that Cynthia went to work. He would come into my room, fondle me, and told me if I ever told anyone he would burn the house down with us in it. Could you imagine how scared I was at five years old, Isa?" Ryleigh sobbed, her breathing becoming shallow.

"You know, you could've told someone instead of killing him!" Isa snapped. Ryleigh buried her face in her hands and began rocking back and forth. She knew this was coming. This was the same response the rest of her family had given her. Their lack of concern, made her feel as if she wasn't important. Like what Isaac did to her was somehow okay.

"I wanted to tell somebody, but I was scared shitless. I didn't want him to kill my mother or my sister!" Ryleigh shouted. By this time, Isa's expression had softened. Remi held onto her hand and encouraged her to continue. Though it was hard, Isa needed to hear the full story.

"Ryleigh, I-I didn't know," Isa cried, feeling sorry for Ryleigh.

"You think that's hard to hear? By the time I was ten, Isaac had graduated to penetrating me anally! The first time he did it, he waited until Remi had gone over to Asia's for a sleepover. That night, I begged Cynthia to let me go with Remi, but she said no. I was so scared that I didn't go to sleep. Sure enough, he came into my room. I fought as much as I could, but I was only ten. Let's face it, I was no match for a grown ass man. Eventually, he pinned me to the bed face down and fucking sodomized me!!!" Ryleigh cried as her chest heaved up and down.

She hated everything about Isaac. He was a sick man who had a fetish for little girls, and at that very moment, Ryleigh felt like he deserved to die.

"Ryleigh, I'm so sorry," Isa cried as she threw her arms around her sister in attempts to console her. She was heartbroken, and though she didn't get the chance to meet him, she hated Isaac for her sister.

"No, get off me! You need to hear the rest."

"I don't wanna hear any more," Isa sobbed, shaking her head from left to right. She had heard enough, it was too painful to listen to.

"No, you need to hear about the night he died," Ryleigh said, pushing her away. All kinds of feelings had resurfaced, and she was no longer in control of her emotions.

*"See you in the morning, baby," Isaac said as Cynthia left for work.*

*"Okay, make sure you have Ryleigh take more medicine in about an hour," Cynthia instructed. Ryleigh was thankful that she had the flu. That meant that Isaac wouldn't come in her room bothering her.*

*"Here, take this medicine and go on to bed," Isaac said as he handed her two Nyquil capsules and a glass of water. Ryleigh noticed that he was rushing her, which was unusual. He stood over her and watched as she popped both capsules in her mouth and drank some water. Once he left out of the room, she spit the medicine into a napkin. Waiting a while, she crept into the living room to see if Isaac was still in his recliner like he*

*normally was, watching TV. When she realized he wasn't, she knew something was wrong.*

*Ryleigh watched in horror as Isaac crept into Remi's room. By the time she got to the door, Isaac was slowly pulling the covers back. Thinking quick, Ryleigh ran to her parents' room and grabbed Isaac's gun off the dresser. She refused to let him hurt her sister like he had done her for so many years.*

*By the time she made it back, Isaac was rubbing on Remi's leg causing her to stir in her sleep. Ryleigh didn't think twice as she held the gun up and pulled the trigger, emptying the clip. Remi jumped up as they both watched Isaac's masculine frame hit the ground. His body had been riddled with bullets and he was now struggling to breathe. Remi screamed for her to go get the phone and call for help, but she couldn't. Time stood still as she watched Isaac reach out to her, taking his last breath. With tears in her eyes, Ryleigh dropped to her knees. Relief washed over her body as she looked at Remi with pleading eyes. Isaac was gone, he would never be able to hurt her again.*

"I didn't know what else to do! He was going to hurt my sister!" Ryleigh sobbed as she slid to the floor and cradled her knees to her chest. "And to think, my mother still doesn't believe me. Do you know how the fuck that feels? For the woman who gave me life to tell me to my face that I'm a liar?" Ryleigh asked, turning in Isa's direction. Isa had no words, she was speechless.

"He can't hurt you anymore, Ry," Remi cried as she consoled her sister.

"Remi, why didn't you tell your mother what he did?" Isa asked in disbelief. If it really happened like Ryleigh said, then surely Remi should've been able to back her sister up so that she wouldn't look like a liar. Remi wiped the tears from her face and looked at Isa like she had two heads on her shoulders.

"Do you think for one second that if I would've known what Isaac was doing to her, I would've let that happen? Would I rather it had been me? Yes! That night, when I heard those gunshots ring out, I didn't know what to think. All I know is that I was sleep and minutes later, my little sister is being whisked away in the back of a police car and labeled a murderer. At that point, what I said didn't matter!" Remi sighed.

"Cynthia already had it fixed up in her head that I was jealous at the fact that Isaac had started showing Remi more attention than me," Ryleigh added.

"You know, it's crazy now that I think about it, because Daddy was always more fond of you than anything. I remember how he would always sit you in his lap," Remi recalled as a fresh stream of tears cascaded down her face. The signs were always there, she just never paid any attention to them. In her eyes, Cynthia was just as responsible for what happened to Ryleigh.

"It was probably in your best interest that you didn't get to know him, Isa," Remi said.

They all sat in silence for the next hour or so, each lost in their own thoughts. For Ryleigh, the painful memories would never go away. The disdain that Cynthia had for her was only a constant reminder of the years she'd suffered sexual abuse at the hands of her own father. Ryleigh would never forget when they took her away.

They took her to the hospital and examined her, and when the doctor told Cynthia and the police that her hymen was still intact and there was no physical evidence of sexual abuse, her mother wrote her off like she never existed. When she tried to explain the nature in which she was penetrated, no one cared to listen. Thankfully, that one overlooked detail would be her exit ticket. The fact that the hospital didn't follow procedure that night was enough for the judge to grant her a retrial, and much to her surprise, the jury had found her not guilty. Several months later, Ryleigh walked out of prison a free woman.

Isa sat there still in shock. She never imagined her father was just as evil as her mother. Two pedophiles having kids. Thankful now that she never got the chance to know "*Issac*," Isa's heart went out to Ryleigh. Her flip mouth and attitude towards Ryleigh didn't help the remorse she felt.

"I'm sorry," Isa said just above a whisper, breaking the silence. She looked over at Ryleigh, who held a distant look in her eyes. "I didn't mean to make you relive that." Isa got up and walked over to where Ryleigh was sitting. "Oh, and don't think I missed Remi saying you're pregnant." She smiled a big smile in hopes to shed some light on the situation at hand. Ryleigh rubbed her stomach with a nod.

"Yes, I am, but don't say anything, Isa," she warned. "And fuck Zay, his ass has been ignoring me since the grand opening. At first I felt some type of way about it, but fuck that. If he wants to be an asshole, he can do that with the next bitch. I'm done playing with him," Ryleigh vented.

"Well, who can I tell? I ain't got no friends and I don't fuck with Zane's wack ass no more." Remi and Ryleigh laughed as Isa flipped her curly hair over her shoulder.

"Bitch, now he wack 'cus you ain't feeling him," Remi countered.

"He is for how he handles his baby mamas, but he ain't wack in the bed, honey." She shifted in her seat, shaking the tingling sensation between her legs as she thought of how he put it down in the bedroom.

"Whatever, yuck, with his ol' brolic ass," Ryleigh added as they all fell out in laughter.

"He is big, right?" Isa asked, smirking. "I don't know how I handle him and that third leg he got." Remi jumped up, flagging her arms in the air.

"Oh, hell no, we will not be talking about his dick, Isa."

"Trust, he's a Perry brother, so I'm sure they are all well endowed in that area," Ryleigh threw in as they sat around talking and eating the food Remi cooked.

"So, where have you been, Isa?" Remi asked her with a

concerned look like the older sister she was. Isa shrugged and brushed off the comment as she got up to go to the bar.

"Can I have a drink, Remi?"

"Girl, you are not grown, put that bottle down," Ryleigh snapped.

"I know I'm not but, I need it," Isa whined, stomping her foot and poking her plump bottom lip out. "I need to just figure out something."

"Tell me where the hell you've been and I'll let you have a drink," Remi demanded.

"Remi," Ryleigh scolded, "she is only eighteen."

"Let her live a little, Ryleigh." Isa watched them go back and forth bickering over her age and drinking like she wasn't there.

"I've been at the hotel, but I'm low on cash so I have to check out soon, and yeah..." She looked down at the floor, kicking her foot across the carpet.

"Well, then you're coming your ass back here. Ryleigh trying to move out anyway," Remi noted, looking at Ryleigh.

"Okay, but I'm not staying for too long, and please don't tell Zane." The sisters only nodded at Isa. "Okay, so Ryleigh, make me a drink then, Ms. Bartender," Isa sang and swayed her wide hips to the music in her head.

"This is why her ass doesn't need anything to drink, she is already high on life." Ryleigh got up and fixed Isa a quick concoction. Isa took the drink and hugged Ryleigh before going to the car to grab her duffle bag.

"I'm staying tonight," she told them both before going to the back of the apartment.

C asey paced the apartment, cracking her knuckles and talking to herself. Tayvin had pulled a disappearing act on her and the kids. The sound of the keys jingling in the door made Casey stop walking and fold her arms. Before Tayvin could get into the apartment fully, Casey was on her ass.

"Where the fuck were you?" she snapped. "You left me here to play Mommy to two kids, and the fact you didn't even fucking answer my calls."

"Sorry," Tayvin blurted out, dropping her head in defeat. Casey didn't notice how disheveled Tayvin looked until she put her focus on her. Tayvin's weave was pulled back into a messy ponytail, which needed to be combed badly. Her sweatsuit was wrinkled and her face had dried-up tears on it.

"You aight?" Casey embraced Tayvin as she broke down in her arms.

"He promised me he wasn't leaving me, but yet he has left us both, and for a hoe," she sobbed loudly.

Casey was familiar with who Isa was because of their run-in, but she didn't have a background on her.

"What happened?" Casey walked Tayvin to the sofa. Tayvin ran down the story of the grand opening to Casey. She listened intently with a bunch of questions. The fact that Zane left his family for a chick who was a hoe wasn't like him. Casey had been reaching out to Zane for the past few days and his response was always dry. She didn't know where he lived now so she couldn't pop up on him and get the answers she needed.

"He over there playing house and taking up for her like we didn't give him kids and happiness," Tayvin spat. Casey felt everything Tayvin said. She had given up a lot to be with Zane. Casey felt she was the second runner up for him, and Tayvin didn't make it, but for him to leave the both of them for some young chick was a slap in the face.

"Fuck it, Tayvin, he's going to be crawling back soon. We still have some leverage over that bitch," Casey reassured her as the kids made their way to the front of the apartment full of energy. Tayvin hugged and kissed her son before excusing herself to go fix her appearance.

Twenty minutes into her shower, she heard the kids laughing and screaming in excitement. Tayvin stepped out the shower, grabbing her towel and wrapping it around her body. She opened the door and was greeted with Casey standing there with a smirk.

"Told you he will be back," Casey whispered, pointing towards the front of the apartment. Zane was swinging the boys around while they laughed.

"Yo, go get dressed, I need to holla at the both of you," Zane quipped. Tayvin rolled her eyes up in her head. She had been missing for a few days, stressing herself out and racking her brain on where Zane could be, and he popped up looking good like he didn't have a care in the world.

"Whatever, Zane, you don't run shit," Tayvin spat in his direction. She left Casey and Zane standing there. She heard them talking but couldn't make out what they were saying. When she appeared in the living room, Casey was leaning in between Zane's legs, nursing a drink.

"What is this?" Tayvin motioned between the two. "Y'all fucking with each other?" Tayvin directed her question to Casey more than Zane.

"Tayvin, really?" Casey moved away from Zane. "We were just talking, relax."

"Nah, fuck that." Tayvin stomped off into the kitchen. She made herself a drink but it was quickly taken from her hands. Zane had the bottle of pills in his hand.

"You need to take these and stop playing. I'm tired of the episodes, Tayvin." Zane shook the bottle. "I'm willing to work out something with y'all, but I'm not going to if you're not on your pills." The spark in Tayvin's eyes lit up. She hurriedly grabbed the bottle from his hand along with a water bottle. Zane shook his head at her. Casey knew Zane wasn't trying to be with either one of them, but the false hope he gave Tayvin wasn't something she wanted to entertain. He was wack for using her feelings for him to his advantage.

"You're not right," Casey stated. Zane told her to shut up and left her standing there. He enjoyed looking at Casey, but every time she opened her mouth, he would get turned off. She was too ditzy and easily swayed. After spending the next hour with them, Zane put the boys to bed before telling them he was leaving. He agreed to come by every day to spend time with them and the kids. Casey was reluctant, but Tayvin jumped when he spoke.

"Y'all keep this house clean too, my boys don't need to be in no shit hole." Zane reached into his pocket and pulled out a wad of cash. He peeled off a few thousand and handed it to them. "I'ma hit y'all tomorrow."

"Your bitch must be mad at you," Casey snapped. Now she was getting upset at how dismissive Zane was being. Zane waved her off and left them standing there waiting on an answer.

"Don't come back until you are ready to be a man and father!" Tayvin yelled to Zane's back. He wanted to knock Casey out for bringing up Isa, so leaving was the next best thing.

. . .

Zane took off his hat and wiped his forehead. It was now August and the weather was blazing in New York City. For it to be after eight at night, it was still fairly hot. With nowhere to go, he drove to his club. He had been in Miami for a few days and had to get back to make sure business was still running smoothly. Zay and Mir checked in periodically with him but he wanted to speak to Isa. She blocked him from calling and texting, which only infuriated him. Yeah, she claimed she was alright and safe, but he didn't believe that shit. Isa tried to act hard on the outside, but she was very fragile. Finding out the news about her father crushed her. He saw the hurt written all over her face. Instead of letting him hold her and reassure her, Isa took off running. The days spent in Miami, Zane stayed in his room on the balcony contemplating how he was going to win her over. Fallon had fucked her up mentally and he only added to her hurt by playing with her heart.

Zane made it to the club in thirty minutes. When he opened the doors, he headed straight to his office. Zane looked over his statements and documents for rent. With Tayvin's name still on the liquor license, he had to get in contact with his lawyer so he could remove it. Now that he was on good terms with her, he figured now was the best time. Tayvin wouldn't suspect it. The sound of someone moving in the front of the club stopped him from looking down at a document. Zane turned to look at the monitor. Zay was walking straight to his office in a hurry.

"Sup, bruh?" Zane greeted him.

"Ain't shit," Zay said as he sat down in the chair in front of Zane's desk. "Niggas went to Miami and shit."

"Hell yeah, I had to get away from all the bullshit going on here," Zane explained.

"Fuck y'all in here doing?" Mir grinned, happy to see his brothers. They hadn't seen each other since the grand opening and with everything going on, all of them had been in their own world. He had just finished handling some business over at the record label and needed a drink. They dapped each other up and Mir took a seat next to Zay.

"I hit our PR agent up to do a little damage control. That shit was bad for business," Zay spoke up, and Zane and Mir nodded their heads in agreement. Mir shifted uncomfortably in his seat.

"You good, bruh?" Zane quizzed. Mir lowered his head and sighed.

"Yo, I got a lil' situation on my hands." Mir ran down the situation with Ryleigh running into him while he was with Dior. He was certain that Ryleigh hadn't said anything to Remi, but he didn't understand why.

"Hold up, she was looking at an apartment?" Zay quizzed, furrowing his brows together in confusion.

"Yeah, nigga, Dior was showing her around the apartment. She didn't tell you she was trying to move?" This was news to Zay. He still hadn't talked to Ryleigh, but he didn't expect her to try and move.

"Nah, she didn't tell me shit," Zay fumed.

"Nigga, you be trippin', how the fuck she gon' tell you that shit if you won't talk to her?" Zane added.

"Aye, I need you to talk to Ryleigh for me. Nothing happened between me and Dior, I just rather be the one to talk to Remi about it."

"Nigga, you lyin'! You ain't meet up with Dior's fine ass and not fuck." Zane smirked. Mir ignored his brother, his attention still focused on Zay.

"Nah, I ain't fuckin' with Ryleigh."

"You ain't talked to her since the grand opening?" Mir asked.

"Man, y'all know how I feel about that type of shit! I told her about what happened to Daddy and made it clear where I stood on shit like that. She had plenty of time to tell me but didn't say shit," Zay vented.

"Nigga, get out yo' fuckin' feelings. You don't know what made her kill that man. Think about that shit, bruh. She was thirteen, that nigga was probably a fuckin' pedophile," Mir explained.

"He do got a point, fam," Zane chimed in.

"Damn, I didn't think about that. Shit! I gotta go!" Zay said as he hopped up and headed towards the door.

"Aye, talk to her for me," Mir called out behind him. Zay didn't hear anything Mir had said. His main focus was to get to Ryleigh. Once again, he had fucked up, and knew he would have to jump through hoops in order to get Ryleigh to even talk to him.

## ❧ 6 ☙

"Where are you going in such a hurry?" Remi asked as Zay practically ran dead smack into her. She was on her way home from work when she saw Mir's car parked outside of the club. She hadn't seen him since the day he went to visit his mother at the women's prison in Virginia, and she missed her man.

"I'm headed to y'all crib. Ryleigh there? She won't answer none of my calls," Zay explained.

"Is that right? Well, if I were her, I wouldn't answer any of your calls either," Remi fumed. Zay didn't like her tone.

"Aight, you got that, shorty." Remi's mouth was real slick, and if she wasn't Ryleigh's sister he would've had a different choice of words for her.

"Oh, I know. I been biting my tongue and I try to stay out of you and my sister's business, but that stops as of today. She's out here pregnant with your fucking child, playing baby mama number three, and this is how you do her? You can play with them other bitches all you want, but Ryleigh is off limits!" Remi snapped, rolling her neck. She was tired of Zay hurting her sister. Even though Ryleigh claimed she was mad, Remi knew that she

36

would forgive Zay in a heartbeat. Her being pregnant only sealed the deal.

"Yo, you don't know what I got going on with my kids' mothers, so don't speak on shit you don't know about," Zay replied, annoyed. Remi folded her arms across her chest and glared at him.

"Ha! You are funny. All of this coming from a nigga who chose to leave my sister alone during one of her most vulnerable times," Remi shot back. The fact that Zay was trying to avoid the situation at hand was comical to her.

"Your mother came into my fucking place of business talking about Ryleigh killed her dad. Then when Isa asked her what happened, she didn't say anything. Fuck was I supposed to do?"

"You were supposed to stay by her side. You left her because *you* were in your feelings. Trust me, I know about what went down with your parents. Mir ended up telling me. But you need to address your own issues with that. What went down with your father and what Ryleigh did are two different situations. Did you ever once stop to think about *why* Ryleigh killed him?" Remi asked with tears in her eyes. No matter how much she tried to be strong and hold back the tears, she just simply couldn't. The past was painful and she, too, had to live with the aftermath every single day. Zay lowered his head and ran his hands down his face.

"I know, man. I fucked up," Zay admitted.

"Unfortunately, I can't be the one to tell you what happened, it's just too much for me. Imagine how Ryleigh must feel, Zay. If she does decide to forgive you, don't you dare force it out of her. I'd advise you to leave her alone today," Remi warned, waving her finger in his face. "Let her tell you on her own time, or better yet, leave the situation alone altogether," Remi said, throwing her hands up in the air and walking into the club, leaving Zay standing there.

Remi hadn't planned on heightened emotions when she decided to stop. All she wanted to do was see Mir. She just couldn't resist the urge to say something when she saw Zay walking out of the club. After all, it was her who consoled Ryleigh the day he left her standing inside of the restaurant after Cynthia's revelation. Zay hadn't answered not one of Ryleigh's calls, and that didn't sit well with her.

"What's wrong, baby girl?" Mir asked with a concerned expression on his face. Zane had noticed Remi and Zay standing outside of the club in what looked like a heated argument and told Mir to go check on her.

"Nothing," Remi replied as she fell into his embrace and broke down crying. Having to hear the details of her little sister being sexually assaulted stirred emotions in her that she didn't know existed. To see Ryleigh so emotionally scarred and disturbed scared her to death. If she could take the pain away from her, she would. Unfortunately, that wasn't the hand she was dealt.

"What that nigga say to you?" Mir questioned, going into defense mode. Zay was his big brother, but he would go to war with anybody all about Remi. He loved her that much.

"It's nothing really. I-I just feel so drained. We had Isa come to the house last night so Ryleigh could tell her what happened, and it's just so hard to see her have to relive that, you know? I try to be strong for her, but I can't do it anymore," Remi rambled, wiping the tears from her almond-shaped eyes. "I hate him! He's not even here but I hate him for what he did to my sister," Remi sobbed, burying her head into his chest. Mir cradled her in his arms and looked at Zane. Neither of them had heard the story, but to see the affect it had on Remi was enough. Zane shook his head from left to right.

Mir stood there and held Remi for what seemed like an eternity. He assured her that everything was going to be okay and allowed her to release her liquid pain. If he wanted to tell Remi about Dior, it would have to wait until another day. There was no way he was going to tell her that he'd lied to her about his whereabouts while she was in such a fragile state.

. . .

Zane stood there biting on his bottom lip, trying to understand what Remi had just said. If she wasn't crying, he would have grabbed her up to ask her to repeat herself. After giving Mir and Remi a few minutes to themselves, Zane came back to the office carrying a glass of Henny.

"I ain't trying to be unsympathetic and shit, Remi, but did you say Isa came to the crib?" Remi turned around swiftly, remembering she had opened her mouth. She swallowed hard, trying to think of a quick response. Remi knew Zane was the craziest out of all the brothers and she would hate to have to curse him out about her baby sister.

"Yea, she came by to hear Ryleigh out, but she was gone within the hour." Zane searched Remi's face for any sign of her lying. "She barely wanted to see us, Zane."

"Yea, she on that bullshit! But check this out, call her and tell her to come to ya crib."

"Zane, I'm not getting in the middle of y'all shit. If it's one thing I learned about Isa, it's she likes to take her space."

"Fuck all that you saying, she don't get no damn space." Zane was waving his hand in her direction. "She wanted to be my girl, so ain't no running 'cus she found out some foul shit."

"Zane, please," Remi pleaded. She was mad she didn't leave that part out about Isa, because now Zane was on a hundred.

"Bruh, just listen to her, give the girl some space."

"Says the nigga who ain't got no beef with his shorty." Zane scanned his desk for his belongings before dashing out the door. The drive over to Remi's house usually took twenty minutes, but he got there in ten and spotted Isa's car parked up the block. Pumping his fist in the air, he hopped out. Zane was illegally parked, but he didn't care. His plan was to be in and out with Isa coming willingly or being carried out. As soon as Zane got to the front door, Isa had emerged with a look of shock on her face. If he had driven the speed limit, he would have missed her.

. . .

Isa's curls were hanging down her round face, her pouty lips were glistening from a fresh coat of gloss, and the maxi dress she wore hugged her petite frame. Her hips had spread from the pregnancy, but that was the only change in her body. Her small boobs sat up perky in the thin material. Isa cocked her head to the side, annoyed.

"Going somewhere, lil' baby?" he asked, walking into her personal space. The Vikor & Rolf Flowerbomb perfume met his nostrils, and he inhaled deeply, grabbing her into his arms. "Why we keep repeating ourselves?"

Isa pushed her freshly painted, manicured nail into his chest. "We aren't repeating anything, it's you and the drama that follows you." Zane saw her mouth moving, but he ain't hear shit she was saying. He grabbed her chin and pulled her in for a kiss. The low moan that escaped her mouth let him know she missed him just as he missed her. Isa pulled herself back to look into his eyes. "I'm not doing this with you, Zane, we are done and I'm serious this time."

"We not done until I say we done." Zane gripped her small waist. "Stop playing with me, Isa, on the real," he spoke with authority.

Isa sighed. "Zane, this shit is draining, and if you haven't heard me talking the whole time we been fucking, I'm going away to college." Isa raised her voice, stopping the people who were walking by. Zane backed up and wiped down his face.

"You keep fucking with me, and I'm not the one for games."

"How am I playing, Zane?" He backed up from her. "Talk to me, don't go walking away, Zane." She chased after him, but he was already in his car with the ignition running.

"Nah, you got it, ma. I'ma leave your unstable ass alone." He spat, "Get from around my fucking car!"

"What?" she said, her voice in a high octave. "You mad at me for choosing me?" Isa couldn't believe her ears. She had gone against her beliefs with this whole relationship she had with Zane. Isa ran to the side of the car, yanking at the door handle. Zane rolled down the window and swiped her hand away. Once she let go, he pulled out of the spot and drove off without a word. Isa stood, looking at his car drive away. She was unable to move from the spot. Her head was pounding as she thought about actually being alone. The tears streamed down her face, making her sit on the curb. Isa wanted to end things on her terms, and never in a million years did she think he would treat her the way he just did. Isa unlocked her phone, unblocked Zane's number, and called his line. She was surprised when he picked up. She had hope yet again, only for him to go off on her.

"Fuck off my line, Isa. I got two bitches willing to suck the skin off my dick, swallow my kids, and fuck me good, yet I'm running behind your dumbass."

"Zane, are you serious right now?"

"Deadass, ma, so go to college while I go fuck my two bitches." Zane chuckled into the line. "Oh, and if you blow up my line, I'ma send my bitches after you."

"I wish the fuck you would, Zane. I'm not no pussy bitch!" Isa found herself yelling in the streets with the phone to her ear.

"I don't know about that, you let your moms pimp you out and Remi fought your fight, so yea, you look a little pussy to me."

"Fuck you!" Isa shouted.

"You already did, that pussy was aight, but I'm on to the next." Zane hung up in her ear. Isa couldn't believe Zane. She decided to call him a few times until he either blocked her or cut his phone off. Isa was fed up and stuck on what to do. Ryleigh was going through it, and Remi was nowhere to be found. Right at this moment, Isa dreaded not having friends. She hadn't spoken to Angel since she found out she worked for Fallon. Isa got in her car and drove around for an hour until she couldn't take the aching in her heart. Something told her to go to the house where she stayed with Zane, but she didn't want to show

THERESA REESE & TASHA MACK

up and look stupid. Isa parked the car on the side of the street. She sat there in silence, before reaching over to check to see if her gun was in the compartment. After she located the gun, she placed it in her lap as she started her car and headed to the apartment she once shared with Zane.

She crept up the street, killing her headlights, looking for his car. When she didn't see his car in the area, she left and headed to the club. Her hands were shaking from the anger that rose in her body when she saw the parking lot was empty. Another dead end made Isa send a text to Remi and Ryleigh.

**Sisters: I'm not coming back. I'm going to fucking kill Zane, I swear on everything.**

Without waiting on a response, Isa headed to where Casey lived. When she hit another dead end, Isa got out of the car and kicked a glass bottle that was on the ground. "Fuck!" she screamed out in anger. Isa grabbed her curls in her hands. "Where is this fucking nigga at?" Isa paced back and forth alongside the car with the gun in her hand up to the side of her face. "I swear I'm going to kill this ol' brolic, big dick having ass mothafucka!" Isa was losing her mind as she shouted to no one in particular. She breathed heavily as the tears spilled from the brims of her eyes.

"Get yourself together, Isa, just go away and live your life," she coached herself. Isa let out a long sigh, jumped in her car, and drove to the hotel she had been staying in. She had to get her clothing packed so she could head to Virginia. Isa chose now to go since everyone had their own shit going on, and her disappearance wouldn't raise red flags until she was long gone. Zane's words had cut deep. She wasn't a fighter and never stood up for herself, that much was true, but she wasn't going to sit here and take his verbal abuse.

Isa prided herself on not falling for a nigga, and here she was love stricken over one of New York City's biggest hoes. She grabbed the last suitcase from her room, returned the key, and rolled it to her awaiting car. Once inside, Isa plugged the GPS in for Virginia State University and didn't look back.

## 7

It had been a whole month since the grand opening at The Perry's Brothers restaurant, and Ryleigh and Zay still hadn't talked to each other. It wasn't that she didn't want to, she just needed time to clear her head and get her thoughts together. She wondered what made him have a change of heart, because the last time she reached out to him, he had been the one to ignore her.

Isa was gone off to college in Virginia and Remi had held up her end of the bargain and worked at the restaurant when necessary. Ryleigh still hadn't told Remi about Mir and Dior, because Remi was currently going through her own thing and she didn't want to add any more stress to her life. When Mir called her up and told her what happened and asked her not to tell Remi, she agreed. She chose not to rent the apartment from Dior because she knew that it meant Zay would be able to easily locate her. Instead, she rented an apartment in Jersey, the last place he would expect her to be. It was further out than she liked, but it was her new home and she enjoyed having her own space.

Although Remi was sad to see her go, she was proud of Ryleigh for making moves and getting out on her own. She didn't miss a beat. She called Ryleigh all throughout the day and even came to her house to cook for her several times a week. She even made Ryleigh schedule an appointment to go see a therapist.

Ryleigh left the doctor's office in a somber mood. She was now in the fifth month of her pregnancy and had just found out that they were expecting a baby girl. She went to the doctor alone, but she felt like Zay should've been the first person to know what they were having. Although the situation between her and Zay wasn't what she'd envisioned, her main goal was to keep her stress levels low for the sake of her child. What was supposed to be a joyous occasion for her was one of the most emotional days of her life. Ryleigh wanted to be excited about the baby, but everything that was going on in her life made it difficult.

Ryleigh pulled out her phone and sent Zay a text asking him if he wanted to meet her for lunch. She wasn't mad at him anymore, she just didn't look at him the same. Zay was selfish and only thought about himself, and that was something she wasn't willing to deal with. Although she still talked to Jaylin every day, that was where she drew the line. When Zay text her and told her that he would meet her, she ordered an Uber to her favorite Mexican restaurant. Since being pregnant, all she craved was tacos and ice cream.

In less than thirty minutes, Ryleigh walked into the restaurant where she was greeted by the hostess. She knew Zay was already there, she felt him. His presence was strong enough to command the attention of any crowded room. Ryleigh spotted him sitting near the back in the corner, and just the sight of him made her panties wet. Standing to his feet, he embraced her in a long hug, inhaling her Versace perfume.

The love she felt for him hadn't subsided, that much was clear. The connection between the two of them could still be felt. He definitely gave off big dick energy in his white Gucci shirt with the matching shoes and belt. She could tell that he had been stressing, and part of her wished she could be there for him. That thought quickly vanished as she remembered how he had basically said fuck her during her lowest point.

"You look good, ma." Zay smiled, showing a perfect set of white teeth. His demeanor was cool, but she could tell he was happy to see her.

"Thank you." She blushed. For the first time ever, she didn't know what to say. Her words were caught in the back of her throat and her mouth was dry.

"Look, I'ma keep it all the way real with you. I fucked up, man. It was inconsiderate of me to react the way I did, and I'm sorry," he apologized, taking heed to Remi's warning. He didn't want to strike any ill emotions in her but as a man, he knew he had to apologize. Ryleigh sighed deeply and held her hand up as if to tell him to stop.

"I don't want to talk about any of that. It's not what I came here for, Zaylin," she explained, the pain in her voice evident. He wanted to reach out and touch her and tell her that everything was going to be okay but over the course of the last month, she'd built up a wall. He knew that touching her would only anger her, and that's not what he wanted.

"Aight, you got that," he replied, feeling defeated. The fact that she didn't want to talk about the situation only confirmed what Remi had implied. He would just have to wait and let her talk to him about it when she felt that she was ready. Even if she never told him, he was fine with that. The empty look in her eyes told a story of a dark past. He had no idea on how to handle that, but he vowed from that moment to protect her at all cost. The waitress came and took their food and drink orders.

"I just left the doctor," Ryleigh said as she pulled out her ultrasound and placed it on the table for Zay to see. Picking it up, he studied it and flipped it around a few times. Ryleigh chuckled.

"Is this the right way?" Ryleigh got up and went to the other side of the table and sat down next to him. She turned the ultrasound right side up and handed it to him. His eyes grew wide with surprise as a smile slowly spread across his lips. He was having a girl. Ryleigh attempted to go back to the other side of the table, but Zay grabbed her arm.

"I miss you, Ryleigh."

"Zay, please, don't do this. I only invited you to lunch to show you the ultrasound."

"You don't think I should've been there?" Zay quizzed. He was trying to keep his composure because he knew he was in the wrong, but he didn't like the fact that Ryleigh had gone to the doctor without him. He had done what Remi told him to do by staying away from her until she was ready. He didn't know that included not being present at her doctor's visit.

"Zay, I just needed time to get myself together, and I still do. I just got out of prison, I'm not really ready for all of this. What if I'm not a good mother to her? What if something happens to her? I just want to protect her!" Ryleigh sobbed as she covered her face with her hands. Zay pulled her into his embrace.

"Shhh, don't say shit like that, ma. You're going to be the best mother in the world. And as long as I got breath in my body, you and baby girl will forever be protected. I would never let anything happen to her, Ryleigh," Zay assured her as he rubbed her back.

Initially, Ryleigh thought she was strong enough to face him, but once again, her defenses were weakened. That feeling of comfort had returned, and as much as she couldn't stand him right now, she didn't want him to let her go. She craved his touch, it was electrifying and awakened every bone in her body.

"I know I should've called you, but I feel like I'm doing what's best for me and my sanity by keeping my distance, and I need you to understand that." Zay sat and contemplated what she had just said and though he was not happy about her decision to stay away from him, if he wanted her back, he had to respect it.

"You moved."

"I see you've been keeping up with my movement." Ryleigh nervously chuckled as she used a napkin to wipe her tear-stained face.

"Always. Plus, you carrying my daughter. I'ma always make sure you straight," Zay said, letting her know that he knew where she stayed.

"What?"

"Jersey, Ryleigh?"

"Oh, aren't you quite the stalker!" Ryleigh snapped as she rolled her eyes upward. She hated how her being pregnant evoked all kinds of emotion in her. One minute she was fine and the next she was crying or had an attitude.

"I wouldn't say all that. Like I said, I'm just making sure you straight." He smirked, causing Ryleigh to slap his arm. The waitress sat their food in front of them and Ryleigh wasted no time digging in.

"How'd you find out?"

"Shit, it was easy. I just followed Remi." He shrugged like it was no big deal. When Ryleigh had first moved into her apartment, she made Remi swear not to tell Mir. She had held up her end of the bargain, but Zay was a Perry. He was going to find out whatever he wanted to know by any means necessary.

"See, your ass is crazy," Ryleigh fussed. All this time, she really thought she was being discreet, and to find out that he'd known all along annoyed the hell out of her. Then, she realized that she would never be able to get away from Zaylin Perry. She missed this part of being around him. Zay was funny and always kept her laughing, and truth be told, she needed that.

"Nah, I just know what I want," Zay replied, looking into her brown eyes.

"How's Jasmine and the baby?" Ryleigh quizzed, throwing a wrench in his game. Jasmine had welcomed a healthy baby boy a few weeks ago, but Zay knew that Ryleigh was being sarcastic. Remi had told her the day she went into labor because Mir left her to go up to the hospital to meet the new addition to their family.

"He's good, Jaylin likes being a big brother. I know y'all been talking, but he keeps asking when he's going to see you." Ryleigh missed Jaylin and wanted to see him also, it was Zay who she wanted to stay clear of.

"Good to know y'all are co-parenting." Ryleigh smirked, making Zay feel a twinge of guilt.

"Come on, Ryleigh, chill out. You know what type of nigga I am. I'ma be present in all of my kids' lives no matter what," he let her know. Zay may have been a terrible boyfriend, but he was a good father and provider. That was something their father had instilled in all three of them at an early age.

"I'm just saying," Ryleigh replied, her voice trailing off. She wondered what they would be like by the time she delivered her baby. She sat and ate the rest of her food in silence, lost in her thoughts until Zay interrupted her.

"I'ma drive you home."

"Zay, I don't think that's a good idea," Ryleigh objected. She knew what he was doing and she refused to fall for his shit. All it took was for her to get in the car with Zay and she would be bouncing on his dick. The pleasure excited her, but the drama that came behind it was a deterrent.

"I ain't on none of that, mama." Zay grinned. He was horny as hell and had only got his dick sucked by Jasmine that one time, but that was it. He even felt like shit for reacting on his anger and crossing the line with her that day.

"Fuck I look like, letting you take an Uber all the way to Jersey when I can just take you myself. I said I ain't on that, Ryleigh. Now let's go," he demanded as he stood to his feet. Ryleigh folded her arms across her chest and rolled her eyes. Zay licked his lips and leaned down closer to her face as if he was going to kiss her. "Notice I ain't ask you no questions. I said I'm driving you home, shorty. It ain't up for debate. Let's ride," he asserted. Ryleigh sighed heavily as she snatched her Louis Vuitton bag off the table and followed him to the exit.

# ❧ 8 ❧

Leah kissed Jaylin goodbye and told him that she would see him later as she got into her car and left her mother's house. Since the day of the incident, she hadn't seen Jaylin. She had been going to therapy and taking her parenting classes just like the judge had ordered her to do. So, when the judge granted her permission to have supervised visits with Jaylin at her mother's house, she jumped at the opportunity. Although she didn't feel supervised visits were necessary, she loved her son and would do anything to see him.

She hadn't talked to Zay and she had tried to call his phone on numerous occasions, but he never answered. She checked his Instagram every day, but the only time he ever posted anything was to promote his new restaurant. She wanted to tell him that she was sorry for what she'd done to their son. Leah needed him to know that she was hurting without him. But Zay didn't care, he just tossed her to the side like yesterday's garbage. Leah had given Zay years of her life and all she got was hurt and cheated on in return.

Pulling up at a stop light, Leah pulled out her phone and pulled up Zay's Instagram page. Her heart sank to the bottom of her chest when she saw that Zay had posted a picture of a pregnant Ryleigh with a caption that read, "*She gon' have my lil' girl, I'ma give shorty the world.*"

Scrolling through the comments, she saw all of the congrats and well wishes from some of Zay's friends and family. There were even a few celebrities who had congratulated them on their baby. That was supposed to be her. She was supposed to be the one barefoot and pregnant with Zay's first daughter, not Ryleigh. She had given him his first son, so it was only right.

She stared at Ryleigh's picture and admired her beauty. What was it about her that he had fallen in love with? Why wasn't she deserving of his love? It was bad enough Jasmine's hoe ass had had her baby. Now he was having another with Ryleigh.

At that moment, it felt like her heart had broken into a million pieces. Zay just kept on hurting her, and she didn't like it. The car behind her honked its horn, startling her, causing her to drop her phone. With tears in her eyes, Leah pulled into a gas station and parked her car. How did she let this happen? The whole time she had been worried about Jasmine was in vain. Ryleigh was the bitch who had stolen her man's heart, and she hated everything about her.

She pulled herself together and picked up her phone. Going back to Zay's Instagram page, she had to check again to make sure she wasn't seeing things. Unfortunately, her worst fear was again confirmed. He had posted the picture an hour ago and Ryleigh was in fact pregnant.

"Okay, calm down, Leah," she coached herself as she pulled a napkin out the glove compartment and wiped her face. She pulled the visor down and looked at herself in the mirror before she went inside of the store to get something to drink.

"Sup witchu, shorty. Here, let me get that for you," a voice said behind her as she was about to pay for her stuff. Leah turned around and rolled her eyes at the man who looked at her with lust-filled eyes.

"Nah, I'm alright. I got it, but thanks anyway." She wanted to

IT'S HIS OTHER BABY MAMA'S FOR ME 3

be rude to him, but he was fine as hell. She could tell he had money, and that's what she liked.

"Y'all women be swearing y'all so independent," he joked.

"That's because we are." Leah smirked as she grabbed her bag and headed towards the exit. He sat his items down on the counter and followed her out the store.

"I didn't get your name."

"I didn't give it," she flirted.

"Aight, I'm Calvin, and you are?"

"Leah," she answered, offering him a half smile. Since her breakup with Zay, she hadn't even looked in another man's direction, let alone give out her name.

"It's nice to meet you, Leah. Can we talk sometime?" Leah looked around as if she were deep in thought. He looked familiar to her, like maybe she had seen him somewhere before.

"I mean, I just got out of a serious relationship, but I don't see the harm in us being friends," Leah replied. She thought about Ryleigh being pregnant and cringed.

"Shit, by the time I enter ya world, you gon' forget about that nigga," Calvin boasted, rubbing his hands together.

"You confident. I like that already." Leah smiled as she called out her phone number to him. Calvin walked her to her car and told her to have a good night and to hit him up if she needed anything.

He had done a good job of helping her take her mind off Zay, even if it was only for a few minutes. Although no other man would ever take the place of Zay or make her forget about him, she liked his high confidence.


"Hey girl, what you doing?" Leah chimed into the phone.

"Just got done cooking dinner," Tayvin sighed into the phone.

"I was calling to check in with you, since you never call me anymore," Leah snapped. She had been calling Tayvin since the day they fought Ryleigh and she hadn't returned any of her

53

phone calls. She was starting to feel like there was an issue between them. She even considered the fact that Zane may have told Tayvin not to talk to her.

"It's nothing personal, Leah," Tayvin lied. "I just been having a lot going on with this whole Zane situation, you know?" Truth be told, she had bailed Leah out of jail and at the time, she was unaware of the reason as to why Leah had been arrested. Leah called her and asked for her help and when Tayvin asked her what happened, she told her that she and Zay got into an altercation and she flipped out. When Zane told her the real reason, she didn't want to have anything to do with her. Tayvin may have been a little crazy at times, but one thing she would never do was take it out on her child. In her eyes, it was unacceptable.

"Girl, you could've still called, but anyway, I just found out that Zay's lil' bitch Ryleigh is pregnant," Leah revealed.

"Damn, really? How you know?" She couldn't stand Ryleigh, but she was always ready to hear some gossip.

"He posted a picture of her on Instagram. I'm not going to lie, I'm hurt about it and I feel like she stole my man," Leah vented.

"Were y'all even together?" Tayvin quizzed, smirking on the other end of the phone. If Ryleigh so-called stole Zay from Leah, then she deserved it. Child abusers like her needed to be put under the jail.

"Tayvin, whose side are you on? Besides, none of that even matters. Together or not, he was *my* man," Leah reiterated. She didn't like the direction the conversation was headed, so she switched the subject. "Anyway, I just met this guy at the gas station and he was fine as hell. To make a long story short, I gave him my number. Girl, I haven't even breathed in another man's direction since the breakup."

"So call him up and get some dick then," Tayvin suggested. She wasn't interested in hearing about Leah's love interest. She had her own problems to deal with.

"Listen, I'll just call you back another time. I understand you going through it with Zane, but you ain't gotta take it out on me!" Leah snapped, hanging up in Tayvin's face. For some reason, Tayvin was dry, and that wasn't normal. Usually, Tayvin was always happy to talk to her and over the years, they had formed what she thought was a solid friendship. On the other hand, she knew what it was like to date a Perry brother, so she gave her the benefit of doubt.

She looked at Zay's Instagram page again to see if he'd posted anything else. As she stared at Ryleigh's picture for the tenth time, she figured that maybe Tayvin was right. Calvin seemed like a nice guy. Maybe she should call him up to get some dick. Hell, Zay had been fucking Ryleigh for months now while she sat in the house and cried over him. Fuck that, she deserved to get her kitty licked on. Her body needed a release after all she'd been through.

Not thinking twice, she hit Calvin up and asked him if he was busy. When he text her back telling her no, he asked her did she want company. It was like he read her mind and made it easy. All she knew was Zay, so it felt awkward texting another man. She sent him the address and hopped in the shower so she could get herself together before his arrival.

An hour later, Calvin was ringing her doorbell. She was nervous as hell, but once she opened that door, it was too late to turn back. Never in her life had she made such an impulsive decision, but she needed this. Calvin walked in and they hugged. Leah appreciated the fact that he smelled good. It kind of reminded her of Zay.

"Sup, shorty. I see you living real nice," he said as he looked around her house. "What you say you do for a living?" he asked, picking up a picture of her and Zay.

"I'm a hairstylist." She chuckled. Leah didn't do enough hair to finance the life that Zay had provided her. That was one of the perks that came with dealing with a Perry. They took care of their women.

"I can dig it. This ya ex?" he asked as he pointed at the picture of Zay. Immediately, Leah was embarrassed. She still had up all the pictures of her and Zay, and it never crossed her mind to remove them once they broke up. Part of her still had hope for them. Looking at his pictures brought her comfort.

"Yeah, you know him?" Leah countered. Zay was well known all over, so she wouldn't be surprised if he'd heard of him.

"Nah, I'on know him." Calvin smirked. Leah gave a sigh of relief. She was glad they didn't know each other because she wanted to be as discreet as possible. The last thing she needed was for her business to get back to Zay. If he knew that she was dealing with someone else, he'd never take her back.

"Good, what about you? No girlfriends or baby mamas?"

"Hell nah, I'ma free agent, baby." He grinned as he wrapped his arms around her and kissed her neck. At first, she didn't think she would respond to another man, but she thought wrong. Calvin was a beast and wasted no time pulling her over to the sofa and burying his head in between her legs. He had brought his A game, and she was ready to forget about her problems.

The next morning, Leah woke up and stretched her arms outward. Rubbing her eyes, she sat up and placed her feet in her slippers that sat beside her bed. She couldn't help the smile that crept across her face as thoughts of her and Calvin sexing invaded her thoughts. After they were finished, he told her that he had to finish handling his business and left. At one point in time, Zay had to do the same thing, so she understood his hustle. Everything about him screamed dope boy and it intrigued her. No, he didn't make her squirt like Zay did, but he at least made sure she came.

She had some appointments lined up for the afternoon, so

she got up and showered and took care of her morning hygiene. Her kitty was still sore, but she needed the money so cancelling was not an option. Since Zay had custody of Jaylin, he didn't pay child support or give her money anymore. The only thing he did was pay the mortgage, that was it. She was grateful for that, but she needed cash and Calvin looked like the perfect candidate.

Leah stopped at the grocery store to get a salad to eat since she'd skipped breakfast. She hated working on an empty stomach and she was trying to start eating healthier. Walking to the deli section, Leah carefully picked a salad and grabbed some cranberries and her favorite dressing to go along with it.

She stood in line and checked Zay's Instagram page again and was startled by the sound of a crying baby. She turned around and half smiled and did a double take when she realized it was Jasmine. Even though Jasmine and Zay weren't together, she still wanted to beat Jasmine's ass for fucking her man.

Jasmine picked the baby up out of the stroller and laid him on her chest while gently rubbing his back. She hadn't looked up once because if she did, she would've noticed Leah staring a hole through her.

"It sucks being a single mother with a newborn baby, huh?" Leah smirked. Jasmine looked up at her and once she realized who Leah was, she rolled her eyes upward. All the years of her fucking with Zay, she had never seen Leah in person.

"It's funny you should talk!" Jasmine shot back. If her memory served her correct, they were both single mothers because Zay wasn't with her ass either.

"Yeah, it's real funny. How you fuck somebody else's man and then he leave you for the next bitch?" Leah quizzed with a raised brow.

"And did! Let's be honest, though, I have a better chance of getting back with him before you. Don't forget how you abused Jaylin all because Zay didn't want your dumb ass," Jasmine shot back.

"Girl, he would never pick your bum ass over me, the fuck," Leah said, waving her off.

"Really? I sure as hell can't tell. Every time your son and Zay come over to see the baby, we fuck," Jasmine lied. Technically, she had only given him head once and now that she'd had the baby, she was still bleeding and hadn't even had her six-week checkup. But Leah didn't need to know that.

"Girl, please, that nigga ain't thinking about you. Especially since he got the next bitch pregnant!" Leah fumed, referring to Ryleigh. She didn't miss the look of shock that ran past Jasmine's face.

"Bitch, you lying, he ain't got nobody pregnant!" Jasmine shot back. Leah didn't say anything else to Jasmine. She paid for her salad and left. She couldn't let Zay and his *baby mamas* ruin her day. She had money to make, but that Jasmine, she couldn't wait to catch that bitch again.

## ❦ 9 ❦

Zay and Mir were on the road headed to Virginia to go see their mother. Zane was out of town on business, so he couldn't make it. The only reason Zay was going was because Ryleigh had forced his hand. She made it clear that she didn't want to have anything to do with him until he grew up and stopped being selfish. He had to admit, Ryleigh was right. He had tried to change but for some reason, he kept regressing.

The one and only thing that she said would help him for sure, was visiting Julia. He didn't want to at all, but he loved Ryleigh. He wanted to change and do right by her and their daughter, so he had to face her. No matter the outcome, nothing would stop him from hating her. The way he saw it, what she had done all those years ago, was unforgivable and he stood on that.

"You good, bruh?" Mir asked, looking in his direction.

"I'm cool, fam. All this shit is just weird to me. This ain't on no kumbayah type shit. I need answers," Zay vented as he stared out the window. He wanted to call the whole thing off, but he promised Ryleigh he would go. He had tried everything in his power to get her back, but she wasn't having it. She had been going to therapy and part of her sessions included talking about him and their relationship, and her therapist had suggested him visiting his mother.

"I'm just making sure. I know this is a major step for you. Shit, you the last person I would've thought would be riding shotgun on the way to see moms," Mir stated.

"This shit was all Ryleigh's fuckin' idea. She lucky a nigga love her ass."

"Damn, sis got it like that? Nigga, you pussy whipped like a mufucka." Mir chuckled.

"Fuck you!" Zay laughed.

An hour later, they pulled up to the prison and checked in. The process was a smooth one and soon, both Zay and Mir were sitting in the visitation room waiting on Julia to come out to see them. Zay didn't know exactly what he felt. Was he doing this just to say he went, or did he really need to talk to his mother and get answers from her? The more he thought about it, the more he wanted to leave. What answers could she give him? She had killed their father simply because she was scorned, and that wasn't an excuse.

The guards unlocked the door to the waiting room and in walked Julia. He hadn't seen her in almost twelve years and honestly, he could go another twelve. She still looked the same as he'd remembered. She had put on some weight and her hair was practically gray, but for the most part, nothing about her changed.

She smiled when Mir stood up and greeted her with a hug, and her eyes lit up when she made eye contact with Zay. He refused to speak to her, and hugging her was out of the fucking question. Mir gave him a menacing glare, and he smirked. He wasn't sure who Mir thought he was and he didn't care how many dirty looks Mir gave him. He didn't want to talk to Julia.

"Zaylin, my handsome son!" Julia said with tears in her eyes. Instead of acknowledging her, he looked the other way.

"How you been, Ma?" Mir spoke up. He didn't understand why his brother came if he wasn't going to talk.

"I been good, baby, just trying to maintain," she replied as she looked in Zay's direction.

"Zay, baby, I know you're upset with me and I understand that."

"Nah, you don't understand shit!" he barked.

"Aye, bruh!" Mir intervened.

"It's okay, Zamir. He has every right to be angry. What I did was wrong, but I was sick back then. No, it's not an excuse, but it played a major part in my mental health. I loved your father more than I loved myself, and it led to destruction. Now, I don't know much, but I do know that you and your brother have issues when it comes to dealing with women. Zay, listen to me, baby. You have to change that. You can't keep hurting women and expect their mental health to be intact after you hurt them repeatedly. Unfortunately, every woman ain't strong enough to leave. The last thing I want to hear about is you or your brother getting hurt by a scorned woman," she said sternly. Zay looked at her in disbelief. How was she trying to school him on how to handle women and she didn't even know how to handle herself?

"I know you probably think I have no place to be telling you this, but I've been there. I was once a hurt and scorned woman and although I regret what I did, I've learned so much about life and myself during this time. I may never see the outside of these prison walls, and I've accepted that."

"Why didn't you just leave?" Zay asked. Julia looked at her son and sighed. She could see the pain he felt from losing his father was forever etched in his mind.

"I tried. Son, I tried to leave on numerous occasions but your father, he wouldn't let me."

"Nah, that's bullshit. You were fully capable of leaving."

"Every time I got up enough courage to leave, he would threaten me to make me stay."

"That's a lie. Daddy ain't never put his hands on you!" Zay roared. He was angry. He knew this would happen. She had every excuse in the book as to why she didn't leave.

THERESA REESE & TASHA MACK

"No, I never said he hit me. He would threaten me and say things like he would take y'all away from me. He told me I didn't have any real work skills since I had been a stay-at-home mom for so long. He said nobody would hire me, and I believed him," she replied. "He made me feel like he was my only option, and I didn't want to risk losing you and your brothers. I wish I would've been smarter. If I knew then, what I know now, things would've gone completely different." Zay thought about what she said and there were still things that didn't add up.

"If that's the case, why'd you try to have us lie to the police and say he was beating on you?" Zay quizzed, furrowing his brows together.

"Because I didn't want to leave y'all out here alone with neither one of your parents."

"You should've thought about that before you pulled the fucking trigger!" Zay spat.

"Zaylin, I'm so sorry," Julia cried, shaking her head from left to right.

"No, you ain't, you just wanna use Mir to get out," he countered as he stood to leave. Julia was full of shit, and he couldn't stand to listen to her anymore. He knew he had agreed to the visit, but this was a bunch of bullshit to him.

"Zaylin, please don't go," she called out to his departing back. He knew Mir was going to have something slick to say, but he didn't care. He made an effort but he still felt the same, and Ryleigh was just going to have to understand that.


Zane was scheduled to meet with Mr. Douglas when he received a text from Zay.

**Zay: That bitch on some other shit, she was in here trying to school a nigga like she ain't kill Daddy in cold blood.**

. . .

Zane shook his head, thinking about when Mir asked them to take the ride to see their mother. Zane didn't want to go and he was happy when Mr. Douglas called him to ask him to make a trip to Miami to talk about the club he wanted to invest in. After rereading the message a few more times, he thanked God he didn't go. Their mother had all the nerve in the world trying to school someone when she was a fucked-up individual. Julia had Mir fooled and wrapped around her finger, but she could forget about a relationship with Zane and Zay. In many ways, the two brothers were alike. Zane and Zay didn't forgive easily and they had low tolerance for women and their bullshit. He sent a text back to Zay, telling him he was going to hit his line as soon as he finished up with his meeting.

Zane's last Miami trip turned out better than expected. He had ultimately come down here to escape the drama from his baby mamas and ended up meeting Mr. Douglas in the strip club. With his club management skills and Mr. Douglas looking to hire a co-owner, it worked out perfectly. Zane walked into the small strip club in hopes of drowning himself in liquor that night, but he turned his nose up at the atmosphere. In the heart of Miami, the club should have been jumping on a Thursday night, but it was dead, filled with nothing but older guys looking to get their Viagra-pumped dicks aroused. Zane sat at the bar and chopped it up with the bartender, Miranda.

*"You know, service is slow up in here 'cus y'all got it looking rundown up in here."* Zane turned his attention back to the washed-up stripper on stage.

*"And you think you can make it jump?"* The bartender rolled her eyes as she continued to fill up the shots for one of the regulars.

*"As a matter of fact, I can, first you gotta fix your attitude, though,"* Zane said, half joking. He hated a pretty chick with a nasty attitude, it was a turn off to him.

*"Nigga, I ain't gotta change shit, who the fuck you think you are?" she spat with attitude while she popped on the gum in her mouth.*

*"I'm sure your nasty attitude turned away a bunch of niggas willing to spend up in this bitch, but what do I know?" Zane threw his hands up. "I'm sure you're barely making ends meet, and before you lie, I can tell because your body suit has a deodorant stain from previous washes and lint balls on it."*

*Miranda smacked her lips and looked down in shame.*

*"See, I'm not trying to come in here and make you feel bad, I'm trying to have you and the others up in here bringing in the bag." Zane took a gulp from his Henny and cranberry drink. "I own a lucrative club in New York, so tell your boss to reach out to me." Zane slid her his business card with his money, finished the drink and left the club. The next day, he received a call from Mr. Douglas about his club. Zane smirked because he knew the bartender would come through for him.*

Zane snapped from his thoughts when his phone vibrated again. It was a message from Tayvin. She had been stalking Isa's Instagram and every time she saw Isa doing something stupid, she felt the need to keep him updated. Zane knew she felt like she was doing him a favor by telling on Isa, but she was actually leading him right to her.

**Baby mama Tayvin: just thought you should see how your so-called girl is living her best life.**

Zane wasn't mad at the words, he was pissed when he saw the picture of Isa's legs draped over a nigga's leg. There were no faces, but he knew it was her. He clenched his jaw and squeezed his phone in frustration. "This girl gonna make me take her head off, yo." Zane didn't respond to Tayvin, he pounded his fist on the steering wheel.

After sitting in the car for a few minutes, he got out to meet with Mr. Douglas. The whole meeting, his mind was on Isa. His flight was scheduled to leave this evening to New York, but with this bit of information from Tayvin, he was making a change in his plans.

"Did you hear me, Zane?" Mr. Douglas snapped his finger at him. Zane didn't want to fuck up this business meeting. He cleared his throat before speaking.

"Yea, I heard you, but it's like this, first, Miranda gotta change her attitude, next, the scenery in here gives off creep vibes."

"When you say *creep vibes,* what are you referring to?" Mr. Douglas had to be in his early sixties, so Zane wasn't shocked when he asked the question.

"I'm saying, it's like this, you got nothing but old niggas up in here, the strippers look like they need the money more than they want the money, so the young crowd, like myself"—Zane planted his hands on his big chest—"won't step foot in here, so that needs to be fixed." Mr. Douglas sat back in his seat in deep thought before he extended his hand to Zane.

"We got a deal, tell me your price and let's get this club turned around." Zane took his hand in his, taking him up on his offer. After they talked numbers and decided that Zane would fly down for a week next month, he got up to leave. Zane couldn't get out of the club fast enough. He held onto his sweat shorts that rested midway up his pelvic area. He ran to his car and started it up. Once he was in the hotel he had been staying in, Zane made sure he had all his belongings. He had packed earlier that day, but he was good for leaving things behind. He gave the room the once over and grabbed his duffle bag to leave. Zane called Remi before calling Zay back.

"Hello," she answered on the second ring.

"Sis, I need a solid, before you say no, don't be like that, aight." Remi chuckled into the phone because she could only imagine what Zane wanted. "I need you to come down to

Virginia, don't worry about the expense and shit, just be at the airport today."

"Zane, what? Is Mir okay?" she panicked. Zane reassured her it wasn't Mir but in fact, it was Isa instead. Without giving much detail, he made it seem like it was an emergency. Remi asked no questions and agreed to fly out to Virginia. With his plan in motion, Zane headed to the airport earlier than he planned so he could change his flight destination and order Remi's ticket.

Four hours later, he landed in Virginia. Remi was already there waiting on him. She sat in one of the metal chairs reading a book. Zane had just seen that Isa was out with the dude in some restaurant. On his flight, he made a fake Instagram page to keep tabs on her. She was so naive, Isa accepted him with no problem. The whole flight he watched her story as she showed videos and pictures of her and this dude. His face wasn't in any of the videos, but he was very present in them.

"So, what's this about, Zane?" Remi asked, standing to her feet. Zane shrugged and tugged her along to the car rental place. "Nah, you better say something, you're not going to drag me here without an explanation."

"Isa cheating on me and I'ma find her ass and fuck her up." Remi stopped walking to look at him with a screw face glared in his direction.

"Fix your face."

"Nigga, I know you didn't bring me down here on no stalker shit. Last I checked, you dismissed my sister." Remi had a point, but Zane wasn't trying to hear anything she had to say.

"Fuck all that, she ain't gonna be out here thottin' and boppin' with these bums as niggas," he said in a stern voice. Remi shook her head.

"Y'all niggas are crazy. I'll go with you, 'cus if you touch my sister just know I'm going to fuck your big ass up and then tell my man."

"I ain't gonna do nothing to her but teach her a lesson." Remi was texting away in her phone by now. Zane got the Ford Focus rental for them. They drove around VSU campus for a good fifteen minutes until Zane saw Isa uploaded another story. When he viewed the surroundings, he spotted the sign to Texas Roadhouse. "Bingo," he said, plugging the address in the GPS.

"What?" Remi asked, looking over in his direction.

"I know where she is. Either you can come in or you can sit in the car, but I'm getting my shorty."

"I told you I'm not leaving you with her alone, so I'm coming."

"Say less." The drive to the restaurant was faster than he anticipated. Zane found a parking spot in the front before he hopped out. When they got inside, he made Remi ask for a table in the back. Zane had spotted Isa's curls bouncing from side to side each time she talked. Her back was turned to them, so she didn't know he was there, but she stopped talking and looked around briefly. Zane pulled Remi to the side as he peeked from the wall by the entrance. The minute she turned around and gave the dude her attention, Zane told the waitress to seat them far away but close enough to keep an eye on her. She wanted to protest, but the scowl on his face told her to go along with his plan.

Once Zane and Remi were seated, he stared intently at Isa's movements. Anybody could tell he was stuck in a daze, but it wasn't from lust. Zane wanted to get up and grab Isa from her seat, shaking her until she could no longer stand up. "Zane, if you keep staring at her like that she's going to turn around."

"As if I give a fuck, I want her ass to see me, she think she low," Zane said with animosity. Just as he was getting up to go to her table, Isa touched the dude's hands and got up, going to the bathroom. Zane got up to his feet, checking his waist band for his gun, then he walked in the direction of the table. Remi's eyes were wide open when Zane looked back at her smiling. He turned back around and sat down in Isa's seat. Before the guy could protest, Zane had his gun pointed at him under the table.

"Scream and I'ma shoot yo' pussy ass, country boy." The dude looked like he pissed on himself. Mad that Isa chose a lame to fuck with, Zane was vexed. This guy couldn't protect his precious Isa if given the chance to do so. The striped blue and red polo made him look like a lame. He had his hair cut down in a low Caesar, and his goatee didn't connect. Zane wanted to hit him just off the strength that he thought he was stunting with Isa. She chose a pair of fitted, dark denim jeans, a white crop top, and white and red Alexander McQueen sneakers. Isa was playing it safe with this dude and Zane understood why. He had hurt her and now she just wanted someone safe to deal with. Zane saw the guy's eyes open wide, just as he felt Isa's presence behind him. She stomped her foot and moved her purse from her hand to her table.

"What the hell, Zane?"

"Baby girl, is that how you greet your man?" Zane looked up at her with a wicked smile.

"My man?" she gasped. "Zane, please, you ended things back in August."

"I ain't end shit, don't play with me." Zane jumped up from his seat in her face. Isa backed up, just as Remi jumped to her feet. For the first time, she spotted her in the corner. "You see this pussy right here?" Zane gestured towards Isa's body. "I'm the only nigga sliding up in this gushy, so make no mistakes when I say to bounce and never look in her direction again, playa." Isa stood with a look mixed with anger and shock. Without waiting on a response, Zane picked up her Celine purse off the table and tossed her over his shoulder. Isa kicked her legs and punched his back in a fit. The dude ran so fast out of the restaurant and to his car, it skidded out of the parking lot, causing Zane to laugh.

"Zane, put me down, dammit." Remi was waiting by the car, laughing at how dramatic Zane was. He had let Isa have her taste of southern hospitality for all of one month before he had enough. The pictures and videos she uploaded to her Instagram were enough to knock her upside her peanut head.

"Isa, don't make me embarrass you some more." Zane placed her on the ground by the rental.

## 🦋 10 🦋

"I can't believe you, Zane." Isa folded her arms across her breasts. Her nipples were poking through the thin material, giving Zane a full show. His mouth watered as he watched her mouth move. Isa continued to chastise Zane, but he seemed to not pay any attention to her.

"You coming back to New York, so let's go to that dorm you stay in."

"I'm not coming with you anywhere, you're a narcissist and you're toxic, Zane."

"Yeah, yeah, I'm horny, protective, and I'm good at what I do, so now that we got that out the way, let's go." Zane yanked her arm.

"You're a fucking lunatic, Zane Perry!" Isa shouted in frustration as he pushed her into the passenger seat. "And Remi, I can't believe you came with his crazy ass."

"First of all, hello stranger, second, I had nothing to do with this bullshit." Remi stressed, "He made it seem like you were in trouble." She shrugged and turned her attention back to the window.

"I swear you're crazy," Isa scolded Zane. He started the car and drove in the direction of the campus. "I'm not leaving, and even if I were leaving, it wouldn't be with you," she told him. Zane tuned her out and drove.

An hour later, she was being escorted from her dorm room with her belongings. "Zane, I cannot just leave, I pay tuition here." She had tears in her eyes. Isa had a part-time job in the campus library and she was enjoying her classes. "How can you just come in and disrupt my life after you basically said fuck me?"

"Isa, stop with the dramatics, you wasn't that hurt. Your ass was out here finessing that weak ass nigga."

"I wasn't finessing anyone, I was enjoying Tony."

"Well, Tony obviously wasn't for you if he ran away as fast as he did."

"Fuck you, Zane, you had a gun pointed to him!" Isa yelled to the top of her lungs. By now, they were in the campus parking lot. Remi had tried to mind her business, but when she saw Isa's light complexion red from crying, she got out of the car.

"Zane, let me talk to her, just get your overbearing ass in the car." Not protesting, Zane left them standing there. Isa used the back of her hand to wipe her face.

"Remi, I don't want to go back there. It's literally nothing but my pain in New York." Remi pulled Isa into her arms.

"I'm so sorry, Isa, and I wouldn't force you to come back, but me and Ryleigh are there and she's having our niece." Isa heard everything she said, but it wasn't convincing enough.

"Out here I have a dorm room, a job, my car, and I just feel independent, a fresh start." Isa sniffed back the tears. "Living up north was nothing but hurt and pain."

"I know, sis, well I'm with whatever, but can you at least come for the weekend and you can figure out if you want to stay or leave?" Remi pleaded. "Ryleigh would be really happy to see you."

Isa really contemplated before agreeing to come along. She made sure Remi sat in the front and her in the backseat. Zane wanted to say hell no, but then he would risk the chance of her coming. Zane's phone had rung for the third time, and after he hit ignore on the phone, Isa sat up from her lying position.

"You gonna answer the phone or keep having one of your bitches guessing?"

"See, there you go, being jealous. That's Zay," Zane said, looking at Isa through the overhead mirror.

"Whatever, Zane, you must think I'm stupid."

Zane stopped short on the side of the highway, making Isa fly towards the front. Her body flew up against the driver's seat. Zane unhooked his phone from the iPhone USB. He tossed it behind him. "The code is my birthday, go through it and check," Zane taunted her. Isa cut her eyes at him. She unlocked the number with his birthday. Without going through the phone, she handed it back to him. If he had given her a bogus code then she would have spazzed, but since it was the correct code, she sat back deep in thought.

The rest of the ride, Isa sat in the back in silence. She was fighting with herself to try and stay strong, but she missed Zane. She missed his hold at night, his scent, and the way he talked. She was sprung and at this moment, she didn't care who knew. Isa sat up in the back seat, stretching. She looked over at Remi who was knocked out, snoring lightly.

"Can we make a stop, Zane?" she asked, hoping he wasn't salty.

"You gotta pee or something?"

"Or something," Isa flirted.

"Isa, do you gotta piss, what the fuck?"

"Forget it, Zane, that's why I don't want to do this with you." Isa threw herself into the seat. "You're so bipolar."

"I'm tired, I'm the only one driving and you playing games." By now, they had reached New Jersey.

"So come with me to the rest stop, stop acting like that." Isa touched Zane's shoulder from behind.

"Aight." Zane drove into the rest stop. When he parked,

Remi stirred in her sleep. Isa lightly tapped her, letting her know she was stepping outside. Remi brushed her off and turned her head.

"C'mon, I'm hungry." Isa grabbed Zane's hand, leading him to the food court. She settled on Auntie Anne's. After she placed her order, Isa leaned up against Zane.

"Don't come trying to warm up to me, who was that fuck boy?"

"Zane, he was nobody but a classmate." Isa stressed to him, "You have to understand the position you put me in."

"Isa, I get what I said was fucked up, but you be on some childish shit, fa'real."

"Come give me some dick in the bathroom," Isa whispered in his ear.

"I ain't fucking in these damn bathrooms, that shit ain't sanitary," Zane told her with a raised brow. Isa was horny, it didn't cross her mind about the cleanliness of the bathroom.

"Fine, let's go." Isa grabbed the bag of food from the counter with Zane running behind her. She was vexed, but she was determined to get some dick. Isa hadn't fucked since she left New York. She walked up to the car, approaching Remi, who was on the phone. "Remi, can you please go get something from the rest stop." She widened her eyes, signaling she wanted to be alone with Zane.

"And do what, Isa?"

"I don't know but I want to fuck, right now!" Isa whispered in Remi's ear.

"You nasty heifer, you got fifteen minutes." Remi reached for the handle to exit the car. When she was gone, Isa climbed into the backseat, removing her jeans.

"Zane, c'mon, we only have fifteen minutes, babe." Zane was looking at Isa like she was crazy, but he was game. Isa had been horny from the minute she spotted Zane in the restaurant. The way he manhandled her and dismissed Tony only made her want to drop to her knees and suck his dick.

"You ain't said shit." Zane climbed into the back seat. "This car small as fuck, Isa, so I hope you plan on fucking me right later on."

"I got you, baby." Isa waited until Zane's pants were down before she made his semi-erect dick disappear in her mouth. She licked and sucked on his shaft until his dick was standing straight up. Isa got up from her sitting position, she straddled him, and slid down on him.

"Fuck, Isa, this shit is tight," Zane said through clenched teeth. Isa gyrated her hips slow and then fast, rubbing her clit up against the head of his dick each time she raised up. Zane used his hand to thumb her clit. Isa moaned and hissed in bliss.

"Argh shit, Zane, damn, I'm going to cum!" Isa said, bouncing up and down. Zane's dick jerked as he held her ass in his hands. He drilled her from under, making her scream and cream on him. Isa threw her head back, trying to catch her breath. She almost choked trying to breathe.

"Yea, this my pussy, right?" Zane questioned, working up his nut. Isa was spent. Zane continued to fuck her until he shot his seeds up in her. "Shit, baby." Isa laid her head on his chest. "I think them people saw us," Zane said, looking at the fogged-up windows.

"I don't give a damn. I hope they heard me screaming too, nosy fuckers." Zane laughed at Isa's bluntness. By the time they had wiped off and finished getting dressed, Remi was knocking on the window.

"I hope y'all nasty asses cleaned up these seats, 'cus I'll be damned if I sit in some jizz."

"All the jizz is inside of me, sis, don't worry." Remi made a groaning sound before hopping back in the passenger seat.

"I'd sit back there, but I'll pass." She turned up her nose to Isa, who stuck out her tongue in a playful manner. The rest of the ride, they blasted music and sang to the songs. After dropping Remi off to her apartment, Isa went back home with Zane.

"You good?" he asked her, grabbing her hand in his.

"Yea, I'm good, but I'm just not sure where you want this to go, Zane."

"Stop stressing the small shit, ma, just ride with me 'til the wheels fall off."

"I pass on that. I'll ride with you, but not 'til no damn wheels fall off." Isa laughed at the serious look on Zane's face. When they made it into the apartment, they showered together. Isa went to go get oiled up while Zane called Zay back. As soon as Zay picked up, he went off on Zane for ignoring him today. All Isa heard was "my bad bruh," "I know,"

"my fault." She tied her hair up and got in bed.

The sound of her vibrating phone woke her from her slumber. Zane's large arms were wrapped around her petite frame. She lifted up, moving his arm, trying not to wake him. He scuffed and groaned before turning over. Isa's iPhone was vibrating on the nightstand with a number she didn't know flashing on the screen. She grabbed it up and answered before it rang out.

"Uh, hello," she stuttered.

"Hello, am I speaking to Isa, the daughter of Fallon?" a female spoke into the line.

"Yea, can I help you?" Isa scratched her head and tapped her foot. She hadn't heard from Fallon since the grand opening, and she was happy. Now with someone calling her about Fallon, she was pissed.

"I'm calling because your mother was brought in here after passing out in a bar. We had to give her fluids and it seems as though she has alcohol poisoning." Isa wanted to say *and*, but the nurse didn't know the backstory on their relationship.

"Oh," was all Isa could muster up. Was she cold hearted? No, but with the hand she was dealt, Isa didn't give a damn if Fallon got shot up. It was her karma, and if the Lord was ready for her, then who was Isa to intervene.

THERESA REESE & TASHA MACK

"Yes, so I wanted to reach out to the family and she has on file. You are welcome to come to the hospital and visit." Isa stopped her before she could go on.

"Nah, I'm not coming, but thanks for letting me know what was up. If she lives, she should learn from her mistakes." That was all Isa said before she ended the call. Left with a sour taste in her mouth, Isa looked over her shoulder to see that Zane was still sleeping. She reached over to the recliner and grabbed his robe. Isa wrapped herself inside and left out of the room. She rummaged through his cabinets looking for some tea and honey. When she stumbled across the tea bags, she reached up to get them, only to be scared half to death. Zane had walked up on her and touched her back. With her mother heavily on her mind, she wasn't aware of her surroundings, so she didn't feel his presence.

"Zane, what the hell?"

"I'm sorry, baby, but I heard you on the phone and I figured you needed me to come and see if you were good." Isa turned around to face him. It was at moments like this that she adored having Zane around. Yea, he was a womanizer to his baby mamas, but to her she just saw a boy who didn't heal properly from his father's death and his mother's incarceration.

"I'm good, baby, I'd be better if you just hold me tonight."

"C'mon now, you know I got you. Why you think my arms so big?"

"'Cus you use steroids," Isa laughed, running in the opposite direction trying to avoid Zane. When he caught up to her, he tickled her until she almost pissed on herself. "Zane, stop, I can't breathe," she coughed, trying to push him off of her. "Fallon is in the hospital."

Zane got up and sat beside her. "What you wanna do?"

"I don't want to see her at all, I just needed to get that off my chest." Isa got up and made her way into Zane's lap. She wanted him to hold her and tell her he had her back and everything was fine. When she inhaled and exhaled, she relaxed in his arms.

"Ma, just know I got you, Remi and Ryleigh got you, and

believe it or not, my brothers got you as well." Zane ran his hand through her curls. "I know life was hard for you, but you gotta let us in, babe. That shit ain't healthy, and you're not alone anymore."

Isa noted everything Zane said. She heard him loud and clear and although she was scared, Isa was ready to let them in.

"I love you, Zane Perry."

"I love you too, Isa, and when I propose to your ass you better be ready to become a Perry." Isa smiled and rubbed her hand up and down his chest.

"I will, I will."

# ❧ 11 ❧

Zay thought going to see his mother after all these years would be therapeutic, but it only angered him instead. It had been more than three months since that day, but the scene still played in his head as if it were yesterday. The words Julia spoke replayed in his head like a broken record, and he was sick of it. Whether he understood it from her angle or not, that didn't change the fact that his father was gone. The only thing Zay could do from this point forward was make better decisions.

With his daughter coming soon, changing his behavior was something that weighed on him daily. Ryleigh was now in her eighth month of pregnancy and their daughter was growing just fine. Although he and Ryleigh spent a lot of time together, she was adamant about them not being together. Since the day of the grand opening, she had become someone else and he'd already made the mistake of leaving her. He wasn't willing to make that same mistake twice.

"Babe, can you come and hang this up please?" Ryleigh asked, sighing heavily. She had been decorating the second bedroom in her apartment for their daughter, against Zay's wishes. He wanted to buy them a house, but Ryleigh wasn't ready to take that step with him just yet.

"I don't know why yo' ass is doing all this shit when you know that you and the baby will be at my crib most of the time," Zay countered, walking into the nursery. Ryleigh was sitting in the rocking chair that she had recently ordered from Wayfair.

"No we're not, Zay! I don't have a problem with you being here, but we are going to do things on my terms," Ryleigh said, rolling her neck. Zay couldn't wait until she had the baby. If she wasn't eating and ordering him around, she had an attitude or was emotional. He was over the dramatics, but that didn't stop him from doing whatever she asked.

"Did you think about the names?" Zay asked, changing the subject. He had learned to just let Ryleigh rant because if he didn't, she would've started crying, and he couldn't handle that.

"No, Zaylin, I kind of feel like, I need to see her face first. I know there were a ton of names we discussed, but I think we should wait until she's here," Ryleigh answered. For once, Zay didn't feel like Ryleigh was being difficult, he actually agreed with her. Zay's phone rang, interrupting his thoughts. He answered and put it on speaker.

"Zay, you need to come up here and get ya baby mother," Remi calmly stated.

"What? Man, don't tell me Leah up there clowning!" he said as he ran his hands down his beard. He hadn't talked to Leah at all since having custody of Jaylin. He made it clear to her that they were only to communicate through her mother, Vickie, but that didn't stop her from calling or texting him every other day. He even heard through the grapevine that she moved on, so he didn't understand why she was still causing drama in his life.

"No, unfortunately, it's Jasmine. She came up here with the baby and she has caused a whole scene. She said that she's been calling you and you haven't answered. And she also said, she's been to your house several times and you won't answer the door."

"See, that's the shit I'm talking about! And you think me and my daughter 'bouta be laid up at your crib!" Ryleigh fussed, turning red in the face and rubbing her swollen belly.

"Chill out, Ryleigh, aight Rem, I'm on my way up there," Zay said, disconnecting the call. "Here, put your shoes on, let's go," Zay instructed, handing Ryleigh her shoes. Ryleigh shook her head and looked at him like he was crazy.

"Oh hell no! I'm not going up there with you. That's your baby mama. You deal with her shit on your own. I want no parts of that!" Ryleigh exclaimed.

"Ryleigh, put yo' shit on and let's go!" he barked, raising his voice an octave. She was close to her due date and he refused to leave her alone. Ryleigh rolled her eyes upward and groaned inwardly as she did as she was told. She hadn't seen Zay and Jasmine's baby yet because Jasmine claimed she didn't want her son around Ryleigh. It didn't make sense to her, because Ryleigh hadn't even said two words to Jasmine.

Thirty minutes later, Zay pulled up outside the restaurant. He told Ryleigh to stay in the car while he handled Jasmine. When he walked in, Jasmine was sitting at the bar with their son in her arms. Remi looked at him and rolled her eyes and continued going over paperwork.

"Look who finally decided to show up. It's a damn shame that I have to pop up at your place of business and show my ass in order to get your fucking attention!" Jasmine fumed. Without speaking, Zay grabbed her arm and drug her to the back where the office was. He was sick of all the drama and something had to give. He took the baby out of her arms and forcefully shoved her into the office and slammed the door shut.

"Bitch, you don' lost ya fuckin' mind coming up here with that bullshit!" Zay started.

"Fuck you and this restaurant, you selfish bastard. I've been calling you to get your son and all you've done is ignore me!" Jasmine shot back.

"Jasmine, I just had him two days ago. I told you I had business to handle for the next week or so. Fuck is you on my line for?"

"Nah, nigga, keep it real. You're busy laid up with Ryleigh catering to her every fucking need like you don't have other responsibilities. I got shit to do, so guess what? You need to figure shit out, just like I have to. You don't get a pass because Ryleigh is about to supposedly have a baby. It probably ain't even yours!" Jasmine shouted.

It took everything in Zay not to fuck her up right then and there. He could see that Jasmine was in her feelings and being spiteful. He never even told her that Ryleigh was about to have the baby, so how she found out was a mystery to him.

"Jasmine, you ain't even doing shit but sitting in the house. You don't even go to work because I foot the bills. I always get my son when you ask me to, and let's be clear, most times you ain't even gotta ask, stop playin' with me shorty! If you didn't have stipulations, this shit would go a lot smoother," Zay stated, referring to the fact that Jasmine didn't want their son around Ryleigh. "Unfortunately, I have other children and other obligations. Now, do what you gotta do and get the fuck out my face," Zay ordered. Jasmine sucked her teeth and opened the door to leave with Zay following closely behind her. He kissed his son on the cheek and picked up the diaper bag that sat on the bar. Jasmine walked out the front door and almost passed out when she saw Ryleigh sitting in the front seat of Zay's car.

"Are you fucking crazy? Give me my son, he's not going anywhere near that bitch!" Jasmine argued.

"Nah, you claim you so busy, right? Go handle ya shit shorty, and I'll check for you later," Zay said, dismissing her. Jasmine was about to get buck until Remi stepped outside. When she walked into the restaurant clowning, Remi got her together quick.

"Girl, you should listen to him. I would hate to have to beat your ass all about my sister," Remi threatened. Jasmine couldn't believe what she was hearing. Once again, her plan had backfired.

"It's all good. Don't even let that bother you. Zay, I'll be seeing you in court!" Jasmine threatened, seething with anger.

"Fuck outta here!" Zay replied as he watched her walk away in a hurry.

"Ryleigh, I'll be over in a few hours so we can go over some last-minute details for the baby shower," Remi called out, going back inside. She had officially quit her job and ran the Perry Brothers' restaurant full time. Although it didn't require her to be there as much as she did, Remi was a hands-on type of person, and being there didn't bother her.

Zay placed the baby inside of his car seat and made sure it was secure before pulling off.

The ride back to Ryleigh's apartment was silent. Just when Zay thought he had things under control, some shit always popped off. It was like he couldn't win for losing.

True to her word, Remi showed up with her favorite ice cream with Isa in tow. Isa was still in school but had opted for online classes instead of being on campus. The way Remi had described it, Zane wasn't going to have it any other way. As long as he didn't hurt her sister again, she didn't care one way or another. Yes, dating a Perry had its benefits, but that didn't mean Isa couldn't get an education and bring in her own coins.

"Heyyyy, sis! How's my niecey pooh?" Isa said, rubbing Ryleigh's stomach.

"Girl, her ass is about to get evicted. I'm tired of eating."

"Don't do her. You better feed her whatever she wants," Remi added, walking past her. She rolled her eyes when she saw Zay sitting on the couch. Since the day Ryleigh had told him that she was having his daughter, he had barely left her side. Remi understood that he meant well and was coming from a good place, but she wanted some alone time with her sisters.

"Hey, Zay, Mir is downstairs," Remi stated.

"Tell him to come up."

"I think he wants you to ride somewhere with him."

"Well he shit outta luck then. That shit's dead, I'm not leaving Ryleigh," Zay countered, flipping through the channels.

"Really, Zaylin?" Ryleigh scoffed.

"Do you honestly think something is going to happen to Ryleigh with us sitting here? Good thing we're her sisters," Remi stated, offering a sarcastic smile.

"Well, Dr. Smith said that she could go into labor any day now and that I should keep an eye on her."

"Boy, we don't care what the doctor said, she'll be fine. Trust me!" Remi argued. Zay turned off the television and looked at Ryleigh, Isa, and Remi. They all had their arms folded across their chest, their attitudes evident.

"Fuck are y'all supposed to be, Charlie's Angels?" Zay smirked, standing to his feet.

"Naw, nigga, we with the gang, now beat it!" Remi shot back.

"If y'all really want a nigga to leave, just say that."

"Bye, Zay!" Isa laughed, ushering him towards the door. "Don't trip, we gon' watch the baby too," Isa added, reading his mind. They had put their plan into motion earlier, and the only way to get it to work was to bring Mir into the equation. He wasn't with it at first because he was tired. He had just flown back in from Virginia, meeting with Julia's defense team. Remi begged him and he couldn't tell her no.

"Aight, damn, y'all annoying, bruh," Zay said, planting a kiss on Ryleigh's lips and walking out the door.

Remi opened up the containers of food and fixed Ryleigh a plate that consisted of three birria tacos with heavy cilantro, just how she liked it.

"Thanks, Rem. I never thought I'd say this, but I can't stand his ass," Ryleigh vented.

"Bitch, you owe me. Mir did not want to come out the house. I had to suck his dick in order to get him to agree."

"What's wrong with that?" Isa asked with her brows furrowed together in confusion.

"Girl, Mir takes forever to cum and my jaws and neck be hurting," Remi explained as they all laughed. The baby started crying and Isa offered to get him.

"You look like you're about to pop," Remi noted.

"Look like? Girl, I feel like a hot air balloon. It's crazy because I just knew I was going to be small throughout the entire pregnancy because it took me so long to finally start showing. I can't wait to drop so I can get fine again," Ryleigh said, stuffing her mouth with food.

"Oh my goodness, this baby is so freaking handsome. What's his name?" Isa asked, returning with Zay's son.

"King."

"King Perry, I like that." Isa smiled as she rocked him back and forth. Ryleigh stared at the baby and contemplated her next words carefully.

"This may sound like I'm being a hater, but I swear I'm not, but I don't think he looks anything like Zay," Ryleigh revealed. Remi choked on her water.

"Let me see him." Isa handed Remi the baby.

"The crazy part about this is that I heard Zane telling this to Zay on the phone the other day," Isa confessed.

"And what was his response?" Remi quizzed.

"He told Zane that he was tripping and that this was his baby," Isa recalled.

"I don't know. I wanted to say something to him about this earlier, but I didn't know if I should," Ryleigh added. From the moment they got back to her apartment, she wasted no time taking King out of his car seat and feeding him a bottle.

"I think you're on to something, Ry. I mean, as handsome as this baby is, he doesn't look anything like Zay or Jaylin," Remi agreed.

"Maybe it's too early to tell," Isa chimed in.

"No, Isa, I'm serious. Both Zay and Zane's kids look very much alike," Ryleigh noted. Remi nodded her head in agreement.

"Well, maybe one of Jasmine's parents is light," Isa offered. Ryleigh and Remi both gave her a knowing look.

"Girl, if your man called it out, I'm certain Mir did too. He probably didn't bring it to my attention because he knew I would tell Ryleigh."

"You do kind of have a point. Zane didn't share that with me, I was being nosey and overheard." Isa laughed. Ryleigh had to figure out a way to bring this to Zay's attention without him getting offended. Right now, her main focus was to attend her baby shower and then have a healthy delivery. After they finished eating, Ryleigh, Isa, and Remi chatted about everything under the sun except their father. Even though Ryleigh didn't have much of a childhood after being locked away, she enjoyed hearing about Isa's.

The next day, Ryleigh and Zay had a baby shower for their baby girl, and they had received an abundance of gifts from Zay's family and friends. At first, Ryleigh didn't want to have a baby shower because she didn't have any friends. The day she'd killed her father, everybody disowned her, so family was out of the question.

It was a small event just like Ryleigh had requested, and the food was amazing, thanks to Remi. To the outside world, Ryleigh and Zay appeared to be the happiest couple, but in reality, Ryleigh was having issues getting over the fact that Zay had turned his back on her.

One thing she knew for sure, was that the baby was going to be well taken care of. Zay didn't play any games when it came to taking care of his children or their mothers. That, too, would be something else she would have to talk to him about. If he wanted them to be together, he had to gain some type of control over his baby mamas. There was no way Jasmine should've been sitting on her ass doing nothing all day with her hand out.

"Who I gotta fuck up?" Zay asked as he walked up behind her and hugged her.

"Nobody, crazy." Ryleigh giggled as he cupped her breast. "Zay, stop it! You're embarrassing me." Ryleigh blushed.

"Damn, what you want a nigga to die from blue balls? You ain't gave me no pussy in months," Zay said into her ear. Although Ryleigh was proud of herself for standing on her word, she had to admit, she was horny as hell.

"If you act right, I just might give you what you've been asking for," Ryleigh said, turning around to face him. Zay pulled her close and stuck his tongue in her mouth and gripped her ass.

"Get a fuckin' room, bruh. Fuck wrong with y'all," Zane said, walking up to them.

"Zane, I know you of all people—"

"We don't need to see a recreation of how y'all made the baby. And when she get here, she gon' be with her uncle Zane, anyway," Zane said, cutting Ryleigh off. Everybody was excited about her arrival because she was going to be the first girl among the Perrys.

"Nigga, you got me fucked up. My daughter is going to be with me. Ryleigh can do whatever she wants. Fuck it, I'll be a stay-at-home dad," Zay joked.

"Hold on, I just know y'all not talking about my niece. Zane, pump ya' brakes because I'm getting her first!" Remi chimed in. Isa ran up to them with a frantic look in her eyes.

"What's wrong, sister?" Ryleigh asked with a look of concern. Everybody turned their attention towards Isa to see what was wrong.

"Um, Zay, I think one of your baby mamas just set your car on fire," she revealed.

"What? Y'all stay inside," Zay instructed as he and his brothers walked outside to see what Isa was talking about. Sure enough, a car was engulfed in flames and a red car was speeding away from the scene.

"Fuck!" Zay shouted in anger as Mir pulled out his phone to call the fire department.

"Ain't this some shit. These hoes crazy," Zane said, shaking his head. Whoever had set fire to his car had crossed the line.

He wasn't sure if it was Leah or Jasmine, but he damn sure was going to find out.

As Zay got closer to the burning car, he screwed his face up. "Aye, bruh, this ain't my shit. I got a new one after Leah's crazy ass fucked up my last shit. This your car, Zane!" he called out, waving his hands in front of his face to clear the smoke.

"Fuck!" Zane jetted across the street to his burning Range Rover. The drinks he consumed made him forget he had parked over there after going back out to pick up the boys. "This bitch Tayvin, I swear." Isa was right on his heels.

"Zane, I'ma kill one of them crazy bitches, I swear. What is wrong with them?" Isa stomped over to the burning vehicle.

"It wasn't nobody but Tayvin, she the only unstable one." Zane tried reasoning with Isa, but she wasn't buying shit. On more than one occasion, she was face to face with Casey, and to say she was innocent in all of this was an understatement. See, Casey made Zane's ass believe she was ditzy, but Isa saw right through her little perfect demeanor. Isa rolled her eyes up in the sky. Every event they had there was always some shit popping off. At this very moment, Isa was mad she opted out of classes on campus and came back here to live.

If it wasn't for her sisters living here, Zane would have had to visit her. Tayvin was looney and Casey wanted to be recognized, but in all of this, neither made this situation about their sons. Nope. It was always about their feelings being hurt, or having a younger woman come and sweep Zane off his feet.

"Whatever, Zane, I don't care which stupid baby mama it was, but they gotta get dealt with tonight!" Isa pointed her freshly manicured nails in his chest. Zane looked defeated, but he knew Isa wasn't playing. Over the past few months, Isa had grown a backbone. The quiet virgin he met was long behind her.

Isa stood up for what she wanted and if he didn't agree, she simply told him to kiss her yella ass. She was in school online and interning for a therapist.

"I hear you, Isa, I hear you." Zane waved her off as he inspected the car. The fire department arrived a few minutes later, putting the blaze out. Zane had the look of defeat plastered on his face. He had this Range Rover for two years and only drove it when he wanted to stunt, so the fact that it was burnt pissed him off. Casey didn't know about this car, only Tayvin, so the process of elimination was easy.

"Whatever, Zane, you can wave me off if you want, but I'm telling you, tonight we are going to that apartment and getting to the bottom of the looney tune squad. What if the kids had been in there?" she asked with a concerned look. Both of the kids' car seats were in the car, so Isa was right.

"Yea, I know." Zane was over the drama. He wanted to book him and Isa a trip, but he didn't want to miss the birth of their niece.

"Go get them babies so we can go." Isa stomped over to where her sisters stood. "Now you know I'm about to go over there and fuck one of them stupid ass hoes up, right?"

"Cool out, Laila Ali, we don't know how well you can fight, and not two bitches," Remi warned her jokingly.

"Shut up, Remi, I know I can fight." Isa chuckled nervously. "I had a fight growing up and my mama had me in self-defense classes."

"Well, still, we don't need you getting jumped, Isa," Ryleigh told her sternly.

"Exactly, so don't go over there trying to fight," Remi chimed in.

"Why y'all clowning?" Before they could answer, the kids were running out to Isa's side. Both of the boys grabbed her hand in urgency.

"Isa, c'mon," Zion yelled, tugging at her hand with Cameron following his brother.

"Y'all are going to make me fall in these heels." Isa tried to settle them down. "Alright, my little guys told me I gotta go, so I'ma hit y'all later." Isa turned to walk away but stopped. "If y'all need help cleaning up, call me."

"Girl, bye, you know the Perry brothers hired some people to clean, and we rented a U-Haul to bring the gifts home." Ryleigh waved off Isa. "Just make sure if you need us, you call us."

"What you gonna do, Ryleigh, sit ya ass on them?" Isa asked as they all laughed.

"Isa, let's go get this shit over with!" Zane yelled from up the block. He had ordered an Uber for them to go to the house he once shared with Tayvin. On the way to the house, Zane tried calling them back to back, but neither Tayvin nor Casey answered.

"Baby, just relax, it will be handled." Isa leaned over to rub Zane's arm. He was tense and she was pissed that these women were still acting up almost a year later. When the Uber stopped, Zane didn't wait for Isa or the boys to get out before he jogged up the stairs to the door. Cameron had fallen asleep and Zion was getting tired. Isa managed to carry Cameron and drag Zion behind her.

In just a few short months, Isa had grown to love Zane's sons. Zion clung to her side the minute he introduced them, but it took Cameron a few visits before he warmed up to Isa. Even with the recent miscarriage, Isa took a liking to the kids as soon as she laid eyes on them. Zion was the spitting image of Zane while Cameron was a mixture of Casey and Zane. He had Casey's chinky eyes and small lips, but everything else came from Zane. When Isa made it to the door, she blew out a breath of fresh air. Zane was in the living room looking even more mad.

"These bitches ain't even here. Yo, give me Cameron so I can lay him down."

"Babe, if they're not here, let's just go and come back later on. I'm sure one of your brothers can watch them while we come back this way."

"Fuck that, Isa, I'm waiting for these bitches now." Zion laughed at his father's bad choice of words. "My bad, little man, look, go find your cars and bring me them." Zane shooed him towards the bedroom.

"Zane, just relax, you act like we are not going to see them."

"You're right, I'm just pissed 'cus these bitches always popping up doing the fucking most."

"I get it, babe, but c'mon, I'm exhausted and I'm hungry again."

"Isa, you just ate, matter of fact, you ate twice."

"So, shit, am I on a diet or something?" Isa snarled before leaving him standing there. Isa stood outside, leaning up against the black metal fence, when the red car that she saw earlier pulled up. Tayvin and Casey jumped out of the car, speed walking in her direction. Isa didn't know what to expect, so she gripped her pepper spray from her purse. As soon as Casey walked towards her with a mug look, Isa cocked her head to the side.

"Bitch, what?" Isa stood in a fighting stance, while Tayvin speed walked in their direction.

"How cute." Casey laughed, stepping to close to Isa. Isa sprayed the pepper spray in Casey's face. Casey grabbed at her eyes, screaming, and staggered back. "I'ma fuck your stupid ass up, watch!" Tayvin bumrushed Isa. She pushed her back against the fence.

"Argh," Isa groaned, grabbing at her back. Before Tayvin could get the best of Isa, she sprayed her with the pepper spray, getting it in Tayvin's mouth.

"Stupid ass," Tayvin spat. Isa rushed at Tayvin, hitting her in her face. Tayvin fell back on the ground, and Isa pounced on her. She broke a heel and ripped her dress, but that didn't stop her. Isa straddled Tayvin, slapping and punching her face. Tayvin was grabbing at Isa's freshly washed and set hair.

"Get off of my hair, hoe, and fight like you mean it!" Isa was shouting in between hitting her. Casey was rocking from side to side, wiping her eyes with her shirt. When she was able to see well enough, Casey pulled Isa's hair from behind, flinging her to the ground. Isa kicked her feet in the air, exposing her thong. By now, Zane was running down the stairs, pulling Casey off of Isa. Isa jumped to her feet, only to fall back down and pass out. Casey's eyes widened in fear.

"Zane, I swear I didn't do anything but pull her hair," she frantically panicked. Zane rushed to where Isa was laying.

"Bitch, call an ambulance!" Zane yelled over his shoulder. He touched on Isa's face, and she was breathing, but it was faint. "Isa, you better not die on me, girl." He heard Casey telling the dispatcher they needed the paramedics. Tayvin was pacing back and forth until she heard Zion ask them what happened. As young as he was, Zane didn't want him to witness this drama. Zion ran to his father's side.

"Isa, Isa, wake up," Zion cried. Zane kept shaking Isa until she regained consciousness.

"Huh." She looked up into Zane's panicked face.

"What's the last thing you remember, baby?" Zane asked, concerned. The paramedics pulled up just as Isa was trying to get up from the ground.

"Ma'am, we're going to need you to stay down there," one of the paramedics mentioned. Isa wanted to get up off of the ground and get her belongings. "What happened?"

Isa explained to them how Tayvin and Casey tried to jump her. With each word spoken, Zane's face contorted into a scowl. "She pulled me from behind, I jumped up and went back down."

"Has this happened before?"

"No, but it's probably because I'm hungry," Isa offered to them. She was helped off the ground and into the ambulance. The paramedics told Zane they were taking her to Harlem Hospital for observations. He kissed her on the forehead and ordered an Uber. Zane knew Remi and Ryleigh were going to be pissed off when they got word of what had happened.

ᏣᏍᏯ

Isa had been laying in the hospital bed for two hours with no phone. Unable to call her sisters, she knew they were probably trying to beat up Zane and his baby mamas. "Excuse me"—Isa waved at the nurse—"can my boyfriend come back here please? I don't have my phone and I know my sisters are going crazy," Isa asked, hoping the nurse sympathized with her. The loud talking from outside her room made Isa chuckle. "Never mind, I hear my sister talking."

Remi, Ryleigh, and Zane walked into the room with Zane's sons. "Are you alright, baby?" he asked, coming to her side.

"Yea, but the doctor said she was coming back with my results."

"Don't worry, you probably were dehydrated," he reassured her by rubbing her back.

"Fuck that, them bitches is getting dealt with," Remi boasted just as Mir and Zay walked in with the kids.

"Remi, calm down, I'm fine," Isa tried to reassure Remi, but she brushed her off. The doctor came in, interrupting the couples talking.

"Good evening, Isa, how are you feeling now?" she asked Isa, looking over her chart.

"I'm fine now, I just want to go home."

"I can understand that. Well, let me tell you about your health so you can leave then." She smiled pleasantly at Isa. "You appear to be healthy, your blood pressure was high and I'm guessing it's that little one you're carrying that's taking all of your nutrients."

Isa snapped her neck. "Little one?"

"Yes ma'am, it shows you are a few weeks pregnant, but I can't give you the exact conception date." Isa shook her head in fear.

"I can't have this baby, I may have another miscarriage. Oh my god, I can't do this again." Isa panicked, hyperventilating. Zane tried to console her but Isa was now inconsolable. Remi, Ryleigh, and the guys walked outside the room.

"Isa, you may not have the same fate this time. You're healthy and your uterus shows no sign of damage."

"But I was just fighting, I was just fighting."

"I understand, but going forward, you need to just relax and take it easy. You're in the beginning stage of this pregnancy, so don't stress it." The doctor took Isa's hands in hers. "You are going to be fine, I'm going to give you some information to a really good OBGYN, okay?" Isa nodded and took the information from her. Zane handed Isa the sweatsuit Remi brought her to put on. After a few minutes, Isa walked out of the room.

"Before anyone says anything, I'd rather not talk about it." They all just nodded in agreement. Ryleigh looked over at Zane to see if he was good. He shrugged and grabbed the boys into his arms.

Everyone went their separate ways home. The ride back to the condo was fairly quiet. Isa had a lot on her mind and Zane tried to respect her space, but when he saw her panic after learning the news of a baby, he was worried. When they made it in the apartment, they bathed the boys and put them to bed. Isa excused herself and went to shower. Her head was killing her from the hair pulling earlier, and she wanted to make sure her face wasn't bruised. With minor scratches on her face, she was fine. She sighed when she thought about harming her baby with the fight. Isa wanted to carry a baby full term with no issues, and she had already fucked up.

· · ·

She lathered her loofa with lavender Dr. Bronner's soap, washing her body a few times. She ran her hand down her sore breasts and stomach. "I promise I'm going to protect you as best as I can," Isa spoke. She stood under the warm water and let it wash away the soap and pain she was feeling. When the water started running cool, she turned it off. As soon as she stopped out of the bathroom, Zane was sitting on the edge of the bed.

"I thought you were never coming out." He offered a sweet smile, causing Isa to blush.

"I'm sorry, it smells good out here." Isa's hair was dripping wet, causing her natural curls to start forming.

"Yea, I whipped up something quick for my wifey," Zane told her as he got up and wrapped his arms around her waist. "I love you, baby, and I would never put you in harm's way. I want to apologize for them two fools."

"It's not your fault, babe." Isa laid her head onto his chest. "I just want them to stop fucking with me."

"Don't worry about that shit. Anyway, I also want to tell you that I got your back, Isa, through it all, aight ma?"

"Yes, baby, now can I see what you cooked? I'm starving." Zane chuckled and let Isa go so she could get dressed. When she got to the kitchen, there was chicken alfredo on the stove. Isa was happy, she made her plate and dug in without looking up from her plate.

"Well, shit girl, you were starving," Zane joked. For the remainder of the night, Isa and Zane cuddled up on the sofa and watched movies until they both fell out.

# ❦ 13 ❦

Zane had kept the kids away from Tayvin and Casey. It had been a week since the incident and he had yet to accept their apologies. Casey was calling him every few hours, telling Zane she missed her son, but he didn't give a damn. They had crossed the line trying to jump Isa after they set his car on fire. He had learned that both of them were present during the arson. Casey drove and Tayvin did the damage. Casey claimed she didn't know what Tayvin was up to, but he still called her out on it because she drove away from the scene. Tayvin was proving herself to be unstable. With Isa in his ear, Zane was starting to think about filing for joint custody, if not full.

He was stopping by the restaurant to check over some paperwork before taking the kids to see their mothers. Isa was in class until later tonight, so he didn't want to bother her with the boys' whining. Zane and Isa found out she was five weeks pregnant earlier that week. She was cautious with everything she was doing to avoid another miscarriage.

"Sup, bruh, what you wanted to meet us here for?" Zay asked, looking up from one of the tables.

96

Zane looked over his shoulder to make sure Remi wasn't ear hustling. "I'm surprising Isa with a trip next week. Ryleigh should have my niece by then, and then we are off."

"Again, what's the urgency in this news?" Mir asked with a raised brow. Zane reached in his pocket and pulled out a burgundy velvet box.

"I'm going to marry her. She's having my seed, so it's only right."

"You serious?" Mir asked, looking at Zane like he was bugging.

"Fuck you mean?"

"I'm just saying, y'all got a lot of drama and y'all ain't been together as long as me and Remi, but you already ready for that shit?"

"Yea, nigga, I'm serious. Shit, my dick been wet for years, I'm ready to give my girl and baby the world as a whole," Zane snapped, not liking how Mir reacted. Yeah, Zane had fucked up in the past when it came to relationships and women, but he was sure about one woman, and that was Isa. Those few weeks away from her let him know she was all he wanted and needed.

"Aight then, let me see the ring," Zay said, talking over Mir. Mir's face was still sour until Zane opened the box. Inside, it contained a Pnina Tornai Deco Love Diamond ring from Jared. The diamond rock sat in between two smaller diamonds. "That shit is fly as fuck!" Zay said, just as Remi's eyes widened in shock.

"Oh my god!" She covered her mouth with her hands. Zane turned to her and told her to be quiet.

"Remi, if your nosy ass says anything, I swear I'ma knock you out."

"You ain't knocking nobody out," Mir countered, coming to Remi's defense.

"I'm not going to say anything, Zane." She was geeked.

"Good, but anyway, let me get up out of here and get these kids to their mamas," he told them before calling for the boys to follow him.

. . .

When Zane got to the apartment, Tayvin and Casey were sitting on the stairs outside. The boys ran from their car seats to their mothers. Zane felt bad for how long he kept them away, not thinking about his sons but thinking about his own feelings.

"Next time you kidnap my son, I'm going to the cops, Zane," Casey told him sternly.

"Man, whatever, the next time ya stupid asses want to fuck up my car, I'm going to snap y'all necks," Zane warned the both of them with a menacing glare. "And if y'all think about stepping to my girl again, just know I'm putting hands and feet on y'all about her and *my child*. And before you ask, yes, she's expecting!" Zane didn't wait for a response before he got back in his car and drove off. When he made it to the condo, he sat out front for a few minutes looking over the ring. His phone alerted him of a text.

**Remi: Can you propose in front of us, Zane?**

**Zane: C'mon, sis, I had a plan. You 'bout to fuck my shit up.**

**Remi: Fine, Zane, do it your way.**

**Zane: I am, you will be getting a call soon.**

Zane killed the engine and hit out. He grabbed the bouquet of roses he brought on the way home. When he walked in the house, it was quiet. He thought Isa might still be studying but to his surprise, she was leaned over her desk, knocked out, snoring lightly. Zane laughed at her while he admired her beauty. Quickly, he set up his phone to record the engagement. Her head was laying across a sociology textbook. The small amount of drool falling from her lip made him shake his head. Isa had a purple silk bonnet wrapped around her head to match her silk robe. The small frown on her face led him to believe she wasn't sleeping comfortably. Zane bent down alongside Isa. When he tapped her exposed thigh lightly, she got up, looking at him with sleepy eyes. Isa stretched her arms in the air.

"Hey, baby, I didn't hear you come in here." She wiped her mouth. "I was all drooling and shit," she giggled.

"Isa Davis," Zane said, placing the flowers on the desk. He stood up, dug in his pocket, and pulled out the box. "As I was saying, Isa Davis, I love you with everything in me. I thought I had a solid female in the past but after meeting you, all of what I believed in changed. I vowed I'd never be doing this very thing, but I can't imagine living without you. With you now carrying my child, I know the timing is perfect. Yes, we just met, but I feel like I've known you forever. I just wanna know if you trying to marry ya boy?" he asked, laughing nervously. When he looked into Isa's eyes, she had tears coming down her face. Her hand was trembling as he held it.

"Yes, Zane Perry, I will marry you," she said as he placed the ring on her finger. Isa inspected the diamond. "It's beautiful," she squealed, jumping to her feet. Zane picked her up in his arms.

"It's a wrap now, girl, you're about to be a Perry!" They both laughed in unison. Zane walked over to the phone to stop the video. He set up a group chat with his brothers and her sisters. Once he hit send, he took off Isa's robe and started sucking on her neck and breasts. For the next two hours, they fucked in every position. When they finally came up for air, their phones were buzzing with calls and texts.

## ✵ 14 ✵

Sitting up at the restaurant for a few hours was just what Ryleigh needed to get away from Zay. The only time he ever allowed her to be anywhere without him was when she was with Remi. She appreciated the gesture, but she couldn't stand the sight of him. After all, it was his fault that she was knocked up with swollen feet and a wide nose. Not only did he think it was funny, he had the nerve to tell Ryleigh that they were going to have more kids, as if he didn't already have enough.

The part she loved most about being pregnant was that Zay waited on her hand and foot. He rubbed her feet without her having to ask. He even read to their daughter every night before bed. Ryleigh was shocked to learn that Zay was so attentive to her. This was the side of Zay that made her fall in love with him in the first place. He never failed to show Ryleigh he was all about her when they were together.

After months of waiting, they had finally started having sex again, and they couldn't get enough of each other. Having to relive the sexual abuse of her father made her recluse. It wasn't that she didn't want to have sex, she was traumatized, and with the help of her therapist, she was finally getting back on track. She was certain her random emotions were driving him crazy.

One minute she was in love, the next she was cursing him out and wanted him to leave her alone. When Zay mentioned this to Ryleigh's doctor, she assured him that this was normal for pregnant women.

Ryleigh had just finished eating her chicken and waffles and was begging Remi to make her some tacos to go. She was eating everything in sight and she couldn't get enough. She had gained a little weight but in all the right places. Her hips were wide and her butt was big. At this point in her pregnancy, it looked like she had swallowed a beach ball.

"Bitch, we don't sell tacos here! You know that, with yo' hungry ass. You better be lucky it's for my niece, because your ass would be shit out of luck," Remi fussed as she gathered the ingredients to make Ryleigh some tacos.

"Thanks, sissy. Look, she kicking now because she's happy." Ryleigh laughed as she grabbed Remi's hand so she could feel the baby move.

"That's right, she's going to get whatever she wants," Remi cooed as she continued to cook. It was past closing time and they were the only two inside of the restaurant with the exception of the hired security. Zay thought it would be best to hire a security guard since both his and Zane's baby mamas acted like they didn't have any sense.

"I meant to ask, did you talk to Zay about King?"

"Um, no, I told you, I'm going to wait until after I have the baby." Ryleigh didn't want to add any extra stress to herself, so she kept her thoughts about Zay's son to herself for the time being. In her eyes, Jasmine was just a bitch looking for a come up. Unfortunately, Zay fit the bill.

"I can't wait until it comes to light that King is not his," Remi added.

"Me either, because that bitch stay in Zay's pockets." Ryleigh frowned. She didn't have a problem with him taking care of his kids, but taking care of their mothers was a bit much.

"Yeah, you need to dead that shit," Remi snapped. Once she

was finished making the tacos, she cut up some cilantro and placed them in a to-go container and handed it to Ryleigh. She opened the container of food and took a bite of one of the tacos.

"Uhmm, this is so good."

"Stop eating, fat ass!" Remi squealed just as Mir and Zay walked through the door.

"Don't get fucked up, Rem. Let my mean ass baby eat whatever she wants," Zay interjected, planting a kiss on Ryleigh's lips.

"Well, the bitch just got done eating an order of chicken and waffles, and did I mention she had two waffles? The food cost is going to be high as hell fucking with Ryleigh," Remi shot back as they all laughed.

"It's all good, baby, you can have whatever you like. Daddy got you," Zay assured Ryleigh, rubbing her swollen belly. Her face had turned a shade of red because Remi was telling the truth. She had eaten a lot of food within the three-hour span of being there.

"Aye, Zane just text me and said to meet him at the hospital in Jersey. He said that Isa wasn't feeling too well," Mir announced, getting their attention.

"What? Why wouldn't she call us?" Ryleigh panicked, rising to her feet and grabbing her phone to call Isa.

"Zay, grab Ryleigh's food so we can go," Remi instructed as they left out the restaurant. Both Ryleigh and Remi knew that Isa was still traumatized from losing her and Zane's first child.

"I'll drive and y'all can hop in the car with me," Zay offered as he opened the door to his car and helped Ryleigh get in.

"I don't understand why she's not answering! What is Zane saying?" Remi asked nervously. The last thing she wanted to witness was her baby sister having a miscarriage. She hadn't forgotten about the stunt Zane's baby mamas had pulled by jumping Isa, and she couldn't wait to get her hands on them.

"All he said is that he's waiting on the doctor to come and let them know what's going on," Mir replied.

"Zay, can't you drive any faster?" Ryleigh snapped.

"You want me to run these people off the damn road, Ryleigh?"

"Nigga, yes! If that's going to get us to the hospital quicker. Do what you need to do!" Ryleigh retorted.

"Baby, tell Zane to let her know we're coming," Remi stated, tapping her foot. She was nervous. Their small family was growing and she couldn't stand the thought of losing a niece or nephew. Cynthia refused to talk to her, so Ryleigh and Isa were all she had. Remi wanted kids eventually, but right now, she wanted to focus on her goals. Ryleigh and Isa would have enough to keep her occupied for the time being.

Thirty minutes later, they pulled up to a gated community. Ryleigh looked around and then back to Zay. He had to have lost his mind. They were supposed to be on their way to the hospital and instead, they had made a detour.

"Zay, are you serious right now?" Ryleigh asked, her attitude evident.

"This won't take long. I gotta pick up this contract from one of my new artists," Zay explained as he entered the code to the gate. Remi sat in the backseat with her arms folded across her chest, rolling her eyes. Ryleigh nervously ran her hand across her stomach in an attempt to calm her nerves.

The houses in the area were beautiful, that, she couldn't deny. One day, she, too, would be living lavish but right now, that wasn't her focus. She wanted Zay to hurry up and do whatever he had to do so they could get to the hospital to see about Isa. Zay pulled up to what looked like a mini mansion. From the outside, the house was breathtaking. Ryleigh could only imagine how beautiful the inside was.

"Aight, I'ma go get the contract," Mir announced as he opened the back door and exited the vehicle. The only reason why they weren't tripping was because the hospital was less than five minutes away. Ryleigh pulled out her phone and called Isa again, still not getting an answer.

Mir knocked on the door and both Ryleigh and Remi's mouths hung open in shock. Isa was standing at the door with a huge smile on her face.

"I'ma kill y'all!" Ryleigh said, playfully tapping Zay's arm. He cut off the ignition and got out the car to help Ryleigh. Remi hopped out and ran to Isa and hugged her.

"Congratulations on y'all's new house!" Remi beamed with excitement as Ryleigh came waddling up from behind.

"Yessss, this is beautiful. Show me to my room," Ryleigh joked. Isa didn't respond, she looked at Zane and smiled.

"Well, I would say thanks if it was ours, but this is all you, sis," she said, smiling at Ryleigh. She searched Zay's eyes to see if what Isa was saying was true. When he offered her a smile, Ryleigh threw her arms around him and planted kisses all over his face.

"Zay, baby, thank you! I love it. This house is amazing!" Ryleigh gushed as she started walking around the massive house.

"So, wasup, you gon' be my girl again or what, shorty?" Zay asked, showing his perfect white teeth. He loved Ryleigh and was willing to do whatever to keep her. She was about to give birth to his first daughter, and that meant the world to him.

"Ryleigh, answer this ol' pussy whipped ass nigga. Got big bruh over here looking like a lost ass puppy and shit," Zane chimed in.

"Did they ever break up?" Remi asked.

"I never stopped being your girl." Ryleigh winked. A look of relief flashed across Zay's face.

Ryleigh was in awe of the cathedral ceilings and bay windows in the living room. She couldn't wait to go shopping and decorate. The kitchen had stainless steel appliances with an island in the center, just like the first apartment she had gone to look at. Upstairs, there were six bedrooms, and all of the rooms were empty except the nursery. Ryleigh couldn't believe her eyes.

"Baby! You didn't!" she said with tears in her eyes, stepping inside the room. The nursery was beautifully decorated in shades of pale pink and gray. All of the gifts from her baby shower were strategically placed. They had received so many gifts that Zay had to put some of the things in storage because they wouldn't fit in Ryleigh's apartment.

"Sis, don't start that crying shit. I can't have my niece coming out on no soft shit," Zane said with a frown.

"*My niece* is a girl. It's okay if she cries," Isa added.

"Do y'all realize that our kids are going to be related twice?" Remi pointed out.

"Aw, hell naw, don't tell me yo' bald headed ass is pregnant too," Zay said, shooting Mir a knowing look.

"For your information, Mir and I have decided to wait a few years until we start a family," Remi shot back, rolling her eyes.

"I got us a house, too," Mir announced, looking at Remi.

"I know you fuckin' lying!" Remi called out in disbelief.

"Nah, foreal, our shit on the next street over," he confirmed.

"Well, what are we waiting on? Let's go!" Remi shouted, running to Zay's car. "Wait, how we all gon' fit? Ryleigh's ass takes up half the car."

"I drove my car, it's parked in the garage," Zane said, shaking his head. Remi was truly a character.

"Mir, get yo' bald headed ass woman," Zay said, opening the door for Ryleigh to get in.

"What? Don't act like y'all can't see how big her booty is," Remi joked as they got into Zay's car. They drove to the next street over and pulled up to another house, this one just as beautiful.

"This is crazy! Like, how the hell did y'all manage to pull this off?" Remi quizzed, getting out of the car.

"Shit, that's Mir with the connections," Zay replied as he helped Ryleigh out of the car as Zane and Isa pulled in behind them. Mir unlocked the door and pushed it open, allowing Remi to walk in before him. The first thing Remi noticed was the kitchen. It looked similar to Ryleigh's, only it had a larger island and more counter and cabinet space.

"Oh my god!!! I love it here." Remi sighed as she sat on the island. There was more than enough space for her to cook and host family gatherings. She was in heaven.

"We gon' come over here for dinner," Zay mumbled, causing everybody to erupt in laughter.

"Babe, you don't like my cooking?" Ryleigh whined with tears in her eyes.

"No, baby, I love your cooking. I was just saying, since Remi and Mir are close, we can eat with them sometimes," Zay replied, hugging her. He couldn't wait until Ryleigh had the baby. Her emotions were all over the place.

"Mir? I'm sorry, I forgot to give you the keys to the shed," Dior said, walking through the front door. All eyes were focused on Dior as she sashayed over in Mir's direction with a smirk on her face. Ryleigh knew that nothing good was about to come from the situation. She now understood why Mir was there the day she went to look at the apartment. "Here you go, Mir. I hope you enjoy all this house has to offer," Dior said, placing the keys in his hands, holding it for a second too long. Remi wasted no time springing into action as she pushed Dior back, causing her to stumble.

"Who the fuck is this bitch, Zamir, and why does she think it's okay to fucking try me?" Remi spat, looking in Mir's direction.

"Baby, calm down, you tripping. This is my real estate agent, Dior," he explained.

"Bitch, don't ever put your fucking hands on me! I should beat your ass, hoe. What, Mir didn't tell you about me? I'm his ex!" Dior revealed as she straightened up her clothes.

"Wait a minute. So, you made me look stupid for this, Mir?" Ryleigh questioned, shocking everyone.

"What is she talking about, Mir?" Remi questioned, walking up on him.

"That day I went to go and look at that apartment, she was the one who showed it to me. When I got inside, I thought she was the only one there, but Mir came out of the bathroom, buttoning up his shirt and shit. That was the same day you told me he was supposed to be in Virginia visiting his mother. Mir knew that I was going to tell you, so he called me and begged me not to because he claimed he had a surprise for you. So, I trusted his word. Remi, I'm sorry, sister, I should've said something," Ryleigh revealed. She hated to have kept that from Remi, and she now knew that Mir was no different. Dior flipped her long weave over her shoulder and gave a satisfying grin.

"Is this true?" She would deal with Ryleigh later, so she directed her attention to Mir. He shook his head and looked at Ryleigh. He was pissed, but he couldn't blame her for having her sister's back.

"Rem, I swear to God, nothing happened. She called me up and told me that I needed to sign a few documents and when I pulled up, I signed the shit. Before I left, I went to the bathroom to take a piss. Shorty came in the bathroom behind me and tried to throw the pussy at me. I refused her and she grabbed my shirt, and that's when Ryleigh knocked on the door," Mir explained. "Baby, you gotta believe that I would never do no shit like that to hurt you. I don't give a fuck about her."

"Well, if that's the case, Mir, why couldn't you just use another real estate agent?" Remi quizzed.

"Because this was the house I wanted for us, and the company she works for is the seller. I know I fucked up by lying to you, and that won't happen again. I just wanted this to be a surprise," Mir continued. Remi believed her man, but that didn't mean Dior wouldn't catch a beat down.

Shocking everyone, Remi ran over to Dior and punched her in the face. One thing she didn't play about was her man. Dior had her fucked up if she thought she was going to try to fuck her man. Dior fell to the ground as Remi repeatedly hit her in the face until she drew blood.

"Remi, stop!" Ryleigh yelled. Mir ran over to them and pulled Remi off of Dior.

"I'm calling the police!" Dior cried as she wiped the blood off her lip.

"Nah, shorty, we don't fuck with twelve 'round here," Zay noted as he gave her a menacing glare. Dior picked up her clutch and looked at Mir once more.

"You had no business putting your hands on me, you fucking hood squirrel. You'll be hearing from my lawyer," Dior fumed as she stomped out the house, slamming the door behind her.

"Ain't nobody thinking about that bitch. She lucky I didn't do her bad like I wanted to," Remi vented, pacing back and forth.

"I'm tired." Isa yawned. She had been helping with the nursery at Ryleigh's house and she was exhausted.

"Yeah, nigga, take Holyfield home," Zay added, laughing at Remi. Remi rolled her eyes upward. Although she believed Mir, she was still upset with him for lying to her. Isa and Zane said their goodbyes and headed out the door.

"Umm, babe, I think my water just broke," Ryleigh announced as she stared at the puddle on the tile floor beneath her.


Several hours later, Ryleigh had delivered a healthy baby girl. For the first time in her life, Ryleigh knew what real love felt like. Sure, she loved Zay, but the overwhelming feeling of joy she felt when she looked into the eyes of her beautiful baby exceeded that. From that very moment, she vowed to never leave her side. Her daughter would be able to come to her about anything. Ryleigh would never in a million years make the same mistakes as Cynthia.

At first, Ryleigh didn't want Zay to be in the room with her because she was scared, but he wasn't having it. He knew that Ryleigh had dealt with some traumatic experiences in her life, and he had no problem being patient and reassuring her that she had nothing to be afraid of. With Isa holding one leg and Remi holding the other, Zay was able to film the entire process.

"She's so beautiful," Ryleigh cooed as she stared into her daughter's gray eyes.

"I can't believe she's finally here," Zay added. If Ryleigh wasn't mistaken, she could've sworn she saw him wipe a single tear from his eye.

"Can y'all give my niece a name?" Mir questioned as everybody patiently awaited their turn to hold her. All eyes were on Ryleigh, but all she saw was her daughter.

"Reign," she replied with a smile, looking up at Zay for reassurance. He nodded his head, signaling that he liked the name. "Reign Marie Perry."

"Yo, I fucks with that!" Zane added. "Baby, we gotta come up with a dope ass name for our baby." Ryleigh didn't miss the uncomfortable look that flashed across Isa's face.

"I can't wait until we get her." Remi smiled.

"Nah, it's over for that. I'm not letting her out of my sight," Zay announced as he grabbed Reign from Ryleigh. Finally, the first Perry girl had made her grand entrance. He loved his sons, but having a daughter had opened his eyes to a completely different world.

Isa cooed over her niece for a few moments more before sadness washed over her, but she wasn't sure why she was sad. Isa had just experienced the birth of her first niece, but nonetheless, she excused herself from the room. She stepped out just in time to wipe the tears that fell from her eyes. These weren't pregnancy hormones, Isa was overwhelmed with the idea of possibly miscarrying again. Zane walked up on her, causing her to jump. With her hand on her chest as she tried to steady her breathing, she turned to look into her fiancé's face.

"You good, shorty?"

"Yeah, I'm just in my head, you know how that goes." Isa

wanted to reassure Zane. He kept pushing her to go see someone about her feelings, but Isa refused. Zane lifted her chin in his hand to look into her eyes.

"Baby, you know I want you to be good, right? I don't need you stressing shit that you have no control over, we good and so is our little peanut." Isa cracked up every time Zane referred to their baby as their peanut. He was very attentive to her feelings, and Isa adored him for that. Ever since the proposal, she had been in pure bliss.

"I know, babe, I know."

"Nah, on the real, Isa, you want to be a social worker and shit, but I won't allow you to be in that field if you don't go talk about your own issues, aight."

"I understand, I'm sorry. I try to not think about my life, but it just happens in waves."

"You ain't gotta apologize to me." Zane kissed Isa's lips, and the sound of Remi clearing her throat caught them off guard.

"You good, sis?"

"Yeah, just had a moment, but I'm fine," Isa told Remi. They all went back in the room and hung out until the nurses told them visiting hours were over. Isa was sleeping in the chair with her mouth wide open.

"Bruh, I know she don't sleep like that every night," Zay clowned.

"Yo, bruh, if she dog tired, her ass be snoring too, but most nights she looks cute sleeping," Zane cracked with his brothers. "You know she working in that stupid CVS, in school, and carrying my kid, not to mention she be running after my rugrats. My baby be tired."

"I'm so proud of her, though," Ryleigh chimed in with Remi agreeing.

"Yea, she doing the damn thing. That's why I want to give her the world, man," Zane told them, shaking her leg lightly.

"Are y'all still going to live out in the city, or..." Remi's voice trailed off.

"Nah, we not staying there for long, but damn Remi, you all up in my business."

"The best for my sister is to get her far away from looney one and two." Remi folded her arms across her chest.

"I got you." By now, Isa was finally coming to. She got up and hugged her sisters and kissed her niece's hand before following behind Zane.

## ❧ 15 ❧

The following weeks were hell for Isa. Her personal life was thriving, but school was kicking her ass. She had to cut back on her already twenty-five hours at work just to stay focused on her classes. Zane didn't want her working anyway, so when he noticed her sleeping more than working at the computer, he made it his business to tell her that job had to go. Isa loved her independence and although Zane loaded up her account with money, she didn't like the idea of just taking from him. She brought the idea to him to cut back on her hours, and he agreed even though he hated her working.

Fallon had reached out to her on some bullshit, but that wasn't out of the norm. What fucked up Isa's head was how she tried to make it seem like Isa owed her something. Isa leaned back in the chair at her computer desk, thinking about the call she received just days earlier.

"Hello," Isa said, placing the kids' plates on the table in front of them.

"You ungrateful bitch, I can't believe I used to give you the world," Fallon's voice dropped with malice into the line. Isa snapped her head back with furrowed brows.

"Listen, you gonna get off my line with the bullshit, Fallon. You ain't do shit for me, and I refuse to continue taking bullshit from you." By now, the boys were looking up at their stepmother in shock. "I'm sorry, my babies, go ahead and eat," Isa assured them before excusing herself. All she needed was for one of them to repeat anything she said to their daddy.

"Bitch, you over there thinking you're living the life now, right? Just watch how that shit crumbles down."

"What do you want, Fallon? You're two seconds from getting the dial tone."

"You keep feeling yourself, Isa, and I'll come and whip your ass all up and down New York." Isa rolled her eyes and sighed disrespectfully into the line. "I was in the hospital fighting for my fucking life and you didn't give a damn."

"Fighting for your life, huh? Why? The demons all caught up and you couldn't take it?" Isa was now waving her head from side to side. "All the hatred you have for me because of Cynthia and Isaac, or should I say Rico?"

"Isa, don't get cute with your reckless mouth, you believe Cynthia over me?"

"Ma, please, you and Cynthia wanted my father, and to think the nigga was foul, yet both of y'all low-down bitches was fighting over him."

"Isa, don't speak on your father," Fallon warned, but Isa was on a roll.

"Fuck that, every last one of y'all were poor excuses for parents, but do me a favor and lose my number."

"Isa, I'm not losing shit, how could you be so cruel? We are all we have, baby. Yes, I was a bitch at times, but I was a damn good mother," Fallon said through sobs. Isa couldn't believe Fallon was pulling this shit. With the pregnancy emotions and her lack of family, Isa wanted to give in, but when she heard the boys in the kitchen laughing, she snapped from her somber mood.

"Wrong, you only had my back until I got of age so I could be your next bottom bitch. You're not all I have, I have a family, a real fucking family, so I'd be happy if you allowed me to heal in peace."

"Isa, don't do this, don't push me away. I need you," Fallon told her, but Isa brushed her off.

*"Well, it's too late, Fallon, you had plenty of time to get it right, good-bye." Isa hung up on her. She ran her hand over her face, wiping the tears that appeared.*

Isa's daydream was short lived when she heard the keys in the lock. She tried to fix her mood, but the thoughts of Fallon seemed to invade her happiness all the time. Isa was mad that she couldn't turn her feelings off like everyone else around her. She longed for love and welcomed it with open arms, only to end up getting screwed in the long run.

"Hey, beautiful, how you feeling?" Zane asked, shooing the boys off to their room. They were in the living room with their toys spread on the floor. Like clockwork, he would go get the boys every weekend. Tayvin and Casey thought they were slick by making him get them over the weekend, knowing he had the club to look after, but Isa swooped in and took care of them at night when Zane was gone.

"I'm okay, I was throwing up all darn morning." Isa rubbed her small forming belly. She was now three months pregnant. Her appetite had picked up tremendously, but the morning sickness always prevented her from enjoying a full meal.

"C'mere." Zane lifted her powder pink camisole, kissing on her belly. "You giving your mommy a hard time, huh?"

"Stop, Zane." Isa laughed, trying to back away from Zane. His touch was tickling her.

"Aight, but in other news, I gotta fly out to Miami tonight." Isa whipped her neck back. "Before you start going off on me, just hear me out."

Isa crossed her arms over her chest. She knew he had the club renovations and opening soon, but the fact he would be in Miami without her was bothering her. "I'm listening, fiancé," she stated sarcastically.

"They pushed up the club opening date. I gotta get out there to make sure shit is going right 'cus my name is on that club now, and I'm not fucking it up."

"I hear you, Zane." Isa turned around to leave him standing there. Zane ran after her, but Isa pushed him off. She adored the boys, but tonight she planned on meeting with her coworker Stacy for dinner. Zane was taking off this weekend from "Top Notch" giving Isa hope that he was going to keep his boys, but it was short lived.

"Isa, c'mon now with the bullshit. You out here acting like I'm saying I'm going to fuck a bitch or something." Zane was now standing in front of Isa, whose face was red from anger.

"Zane, please miss me with the dramatics—" Before she could continue, he cut her off mid-sentence.

"Dramatics, you the one over here bitching 'cus I gotta go work. Who you think paying all these bills in this bitch?"

"Ha, that's what this is about, huh? Bills that you wanted to fucking pay. You make me cut my hours at work so you can feed your bruised ego because I had my own money. Now you want to stand here and complain because you're being the fucking man of the house."

"Isa, I'm telling you right now you better check yaself," he boasted, turning away from her. "You knew what type of nigga I was before you got with me, so if you can't handle it, then go," Zane warned her. He didn't look in Isa's direction when he spoke, or he would have seen the tears falling down her face.

"You know what, Zane, fuck it. I will not sit here and get treated like I don't offer anything!" Isa stormed off into the room. She had hoped Zane would follow behind her, but he didn't. She rummaged through her drawers and closet for a few outfits. If he wanted her to bow to him, she was leaving. Isa vowed she would never feel like she wasn't wanted in her own home ever again. She pulled on a pair of gray leggings, her black and gray UGGs, and a Nike pullover hoodie. Isa pulled her wild curls into a messy ponytail. The pregnancy mixed with her prenatal pills had her hair growing full and healthy. She applied a coat of lip gloss and put on her Grace Rudsak coat. Isa texted Casey to see where she was so she could drop off the kids. There wasn't any sense in leaving them behind when Zane had plans. When Isa came out of the bedroom carrying her Louis Vuitton Damier duffle, Zane hopped to his feet.

"Fuck is you doing, Isa?" Zane asked, putting the blunt from in between his fingers into the ashtray.

"I'm not staying here with your self-centered, arrogant, disrespectful ass." She let all of that out in one breath.

"Go put that shit back, you're not going anywhere!" Zane tugged at her luggage. Isa yanked it back from him, stumbling and falling back onto the sofa.

"This is what the fuck I'm talking about." Zane ran to Isa to make sure she was good. Isa slapped his hand away from her. "Calm your feisty ass down. Shit, you and your sisters always on that headstrong bullshit, not this time."

"No, 'cus you don't care, you only care about paying these bills, your sons, and the baby I'm carrying." Isa sobbed, "You don't care about me!" Zane ran his hand down his face in frustration.

"You letting these fucking emotions get to you, yo. If I didn't care about you, I wouldn't have asked ya stupid ass to marry me."

"Now I'm stupid, Zane?"

"Is that all ya bubble head ass heard?" Zane looked at Isa. "You really starting to piss me off acting like I don't give a damn. I came in here calling you beautiful and shit, and the minute I tell you about my business move, you spazz out."

"No, Zane, you think I'm your baby sitter, and although I love the boys, I need a weekend to myself too."

"So say that then, don't go making it seem like I'm acting different or out here cheating on you."

"Zane, I'm hot and Casey already texted me to let me know I can drop off the boys."

"Drop them off to where? I don't want you around them

bitches."

Isa cut her eyes at Zane. "I'm not getting out of the car, Zane." Zane looked skeptical, but he had to head to the airport so he could make his flight.

"Call Remi to ride with you, yo," Zane warned her.

"No, Zane, I am not a kid, and I wish y'all would stop treating me as such." Isa got up, removed her coat and headed to get the boys together.

"Nobody said you was a kid, but you know how they get down!" Zane yelled to the back of the apartment.

As soon as the kids were dressed and ready to go, Isa kissed Zane and made him promise to call her as soon as he landed. He agreed and they were out the door.


On the drive to the salon, Isa was thinking about Zane's warnings. He was so overprotective of her that it drove her crazy. She wanted to prove to everyone she could handle her own if given the chance. The fight she had with Tayvin and Casey obviously wasn't enough to make them believe she had it handled. She pulled up to the salon and looked around to make sure no one was lurking. Isa sent a text to Casey letting her know she was outside in her car. Isa reached in her glove compartment and grabbed her gun.

"Are y'all ready?" Isa asked the boys, looking over the driver's seat.

"No," Zion whined. "I want to stay with you."

"I know, handsome, but I'm going to be busy." Isa frowned at his pout. She looked down at her phone to make sure she didn't miss a text from Casey. When more than five minutes passed, Isa got out the car with the boys in search of Casey. The chiming from the salon's door alerted the receptionist of a visitor. It was now after seven, so they were closed for walk-ins.

"Can I help you?"

"Umm, yes I'm here for Casey. She told me to meet her here

with her son," Isa told her in a sweet voice while looking around for Casey.

"Oh, she's at the wash bowl. I can take you back there." Isa followed the girl to the back while holding the boys' hands. "Casey, your son is here."

Isa looked at Leah and Casey, making sure neither of them were on no bullshit.

"I thought you were bringing them a little later," Casey said with an attitude.

"No, I'm going to be busy, so here they are." Isa sat them up in the chairs closest to Casey.

"Well, I can't watch them if I'm getting my hair done. You and your man wanted them every weekend, so figure it out."

"Me and my fiancé are busy, if you didn't hear me the first time. You and Tayvin be really acting stupid for no damn reason." By now, the females in the shop were looking in on the drama.

"Don't talk about my girl Tayvin and she ain't here to back up her shit," Leah chimed in.

"I'm not even going to get started on you, Leah, so mind your business and keep doing your job." Isa rolled her eyes at Leah. "Now, Casey, I set them up with snacks and their tablets." Isa turned to the boys. "I'll see y'all soon, love you, stepmommy's babies." Isa kissed their cheeks.

"Don't put ya lips on my son, Isa, you out here sucking dick and shit."

"Well it's better than eating the pussy that my fiancé's dick used to go in." Isa smirked as the women gasped before she walked back out of the salon. She headed to BBQ's to meet Stacy just in time for them to get seated before the night crowd showed up.

"Hey, girl," Stacy greeted. Isa smiled before hugging her newfound friend.

"Sup, mama." Isa followed her to the booth. "I needed this," Isa made note of, just as they caught up on girl talk.

## ❧ 16 ❧

"I can't believe you let that bitch willingly be around your son," Leah spoke, rinsing Casey's hair.

"Yeah, well your son is around his father's girlfriend as well." Casey rolled her eyes at Leah. She knew something was off with Leah, but she couldn't place it. What she did know was that Leah could do some hair. Her motive of going to the shop was to brag about her and Tayvin going out. She wasn't expecting Isa to text her and tell her she was bringing her the boys.

"Whatever, Casey, at least I ain't stupid enough to play sister wife to a nigga who don't even want me."

"Bitch, now I see why Tayvin ain't fucking with your old grimy ass. You got a lot to say about other people's shit, but your life is far from perfect." Leah had stopped prepping Casey's hair for the blow dryer.

"Excuse me?"

"You heard me, Tayvin ain't fucking with you and you should have been felt that shit."

Leah was biting her lip, looking perplexed. "She told you this? I didn't do shit to her."

"You right, you didn't do anything to her, it's what you did to Jaylin." Casey shrugged as Leah dropped the subject. Casey didn't want to air out Leah's business, but when she started attacking her lifestyle she opted to put her on blast. Casey had heard about Leah hitting her son and was disgusted in knowing she would do that to get Zay's attention. Casey loved her son more than anything and couldn't even fathom why she would harm hers.

After Leah finished Casey's hair, she paid her and grabbed the boys to head home. As soon as she parked and stepped in the house, she saw that Tayvin had cooked for them. The lights were low and it smelled like the champagne toast candle from Bath and Body Works. "Tay," Casey called out to her. When she didn't get an answer, she called out to her again in a panic. Tayvin was lying in the bed face down. Casey touched her back, but she didn't move. Casey shook her, making Tayvin pop her head up.

"Tayvin." Casey sat beside her. "What's wrong, are you okay?"

"No, I'm losing myself. Casey, just take Zion and go to your house, please." Tayvin's eyes had a faraway look in them. "Don't question me, Casey, just please listen to me." Casey did as she was told. Once she was in the car, she dialed Zane's number. His phone rang out. Casey sucked her teeth, calling him over and over with the same outcome. She banged her hand on the steering wheel before leaving him a message.

"Listen, Zane, I don't give a fuck what you or Isa are doing, but you need to call Tayvin or come bring your ass to the house, it's an emergency." With that, she hung up and turned back around to the apartment. Casey wanted to leave her like she said, but the nurturer in her told her to go comfort Tayvin. As much as Tayvin couldn't stand Leah right now, she knew they had known each other for years, so she would know what to do. She dialed up Leah's number and told her to meet her at the house, it was urgent. Thankfully, Leah had agreed.

. . .

Leah made it to Tayvin's in less than thirty minutes. At first, she started not to go because of the statement Casey had made about Tayvin not really wanting to fuck with her. She had to admit, Tayvin had been acting a little off lately, but Leah also knew she was going through it with Zane. Surely, if Tayvin felt some type of way, Leah trusted that she would be woman enough to speak on it.

Leah didn't know Casey all that well, and she had already determined that she didn't like her. She had some fucking nerve coming to her job speaking on something she knew nothing about. Just because their kids' fathers were brothers didn't give her the right to throw up the fact that Zay had her son around that bitch Ryleigh.

"Thanks for coming, Leah, you were the only person I could think to call besides Zane," Casey said as she opened the door, allowing her to step inside.

"Yeah, whatever, where is Tayvin?" Leah asked with an attitude, brushing past her.

"She's back there in her bedroom." Leah wasted no time heading to the back to see what was going on with Tayvin. When she walked into the room, Tayvin had a faraway look in her eyes.

"Tayvin?" Leah softly called out. When she didn't answer, Leah tiptoed over to the bed and waved her hand in front of Tayvin's face.

"What the fuck do you want?" Tayvin snapped, shocking Leah.

"Casey called me and asked me to come check on you, friend. What's going on?" Tayvin got up off the bed and laughed like she was crazy.

"What's going on? I gave my heart to a nigga who don't give a fuck about me! Everything is wrong!" Tayvin sobbed. "Not only did he have a baby on me and hide it from, he left me for an eighteen-year-old little girl, and now he claims the bitch is pregnant. He's never going to come back to me!" Leah felt her pain. She, too, was in the same predicament. Zay had also had a baby on her and then left her to be with Ryleigh, who had just recently had his baby as well. Typical Perry brother shit. Leah ran over to Tayvin and attempted to console her.

"Don't you fucking touch me, bitch! Don't think Zane ain't tell me about that bullshit you pulled with Jaylin. I should kick your ass! And Casey, I don't care what I got going on, you were wrong to call this bitch and bring her into my house!" Tayvin frowned, pointing her finger at Casey.

"Tayvin, I didn't know what else to do. I-I tried to call Zane but he wouldn't answer the phone," Casey tried to explain.

"You got a problem with me, Tayvin, why didn't you just come to me about it?" Leah quizzed with her arms folded across her chest.

"Let me tell you something, I don't owe you any explanations. You know what you did was wrong. Now get the fuck out of my house!" Tayvin snapped, pointing towards the door. "I don't need you or no other bitch checking up on me, fuck y'all!" Casey was hurt. All she had done was try to help, and this wasn't the outcome she was expecting. She grabbed both of the boys and left. She was done trying to help Tayvin. Leah wanted to say something slick to her but decided against it. Tayvin was a loose cannon, so she decided to leave well enough alone. She glanced at her one more time before finally deciding to leave.

Later on that night, Leah called Jaylin to see what he was up to. They still had their supervised visits every weekend, but that just wasn't enough. She missed her son and wanted him home. She had unofficially moved on with Calvin, but all they did was have sex. He never really took her out on dates like Zay used to, and she needed more from him. He was on his way over to her house and she decided that she would talk to him about it and tell him her true feelings.

"Hey man, what you up to?"

"Nothing, Mommy, look at my new room." Jaylin beamed with excitement as he showed Leah around his large room.

"Your new room?"

"Yes, my daddy just got us a new house and it's real big," Jaylin said as he started walking around the house, showing her each room. "And this my sister's room." Leah paused the FaceTime call and logged onto Instagram and went straight to Zay's page. Her heart sank when she saw that he had posted a picture of him, Ryleigh, Jaylin, and the new baby all standing in front of a big beautiful home like they were a big happy family.

"You wanna see my sister Reign?"

"That's nice, baby, let Mommy call you back. I have another call I need to take," Leah said, ending the call. She couldn't stand it anymore. Zay had really moved on from her. At one point, she thought he would come running back to her, but she now knew that he never would. It had been close to a year and Ryleigh had already gotten the house and baby. There was only one thing left for him to do, and that was to propose.

Leah ran to the bathroom and attempted to pull herself together before Calvin came. Suddenly, she wasn't in the mood for dick. Zay had her fucked up if he thought he could just take Jaylin away from her and live happily ever after with Ryleigh like she was his mother. Leah couldn't let that happen.

"Aye, shorty, you in here?" Calvin called out, scaring her half to death. She had been so deep in thought that she hadn't heard him knock on the door.

"Hold on one minute. I'm in the bathroom," Leah answered, splashing cold water on her face. She had to figure out a way to tell Calvin that she was no longer in the mood to have company.

Drying her face with a towel, Leah trudged out the bathroom and walked into the living room. Calvin had his back turned to her, so he didn't hear or see her standing behind him.

"Calvin, what are you doing?"

"This nigga still got you cryin' over his weak ass." Calvin smirked, tossing her phone down on the counter.

"That's none of your business," Leah snapped as she grabbed her phone and stuffed it in her back pocket.

"I mean, I'm saying, shorty. We been fucking around for months now. Shit, I thought you was over the nigga," Calvin said.

"Calvin, I really don't want to talk about that. Matter of fact, I think we should call it a night. I'm not really in the mood for company tonight," Leah announced.

"Why, 'cus that nigga had a baby with Ryleigh and bought her a house? Let me guess, that should've been you, huh?" Calvin said, shocking her. How did he know who Ryleigh was? Then it hit her. Calvin was the person in the picture Tayvin had sent her months ago. Something in his tone made the hairs on the back of her neck stand up.

"H-How do you know about Ryleigh?" Leah stammered, backing into the wall.

"Shit, I was fucking with Ryleigh first. Then this nigga came along and she act like she ain't know a nigga no more," Calvin revealed, as he pointed at the picture of Zay that hung above her head. Leah didn't know how to process the information she had just received. She figured it would be best to use it to her advantage.

"I fucking hate that bitch. If it wasn't for her, I would still have my family," Leah stated with venom lacing her voice. "I can't wait to catch that bitch by herself again," Leah vented, not caring that she was talking to Calvin. Ryleigh had taken every-thing from her.

"Hold on, Ryleigh did do me wrong, but I can't let you touch her. Now, that nigga she fuckin' with can go, but she's off limits," Calvin explained as he briefly told her about the night he was with Ryleigh and Zay had shown up, forcing her to leave with him. He would never admit it out loud, but that had been a huge blow to his ego.

"What if I told you I knew something that could put him away for a very long time?" Leah asked, the wheels in her head already turning. "That way, you can have your precious little Ryleigh all to yourself, and I can get my son back."

"What you mean? What kind of information you got on him?"

"Does it really matter, baby? Just think of how happy you're going to be once he's no longer in the picture," Leah taunted as she massaged Calvin's dick through his jeans.

"I don't know. I got a lot going on, and I ain't trying to be mixed up in no bullshit," Calvin objected. She hurriedly dropped to her knees and unbuckled his belt. If she was going to use Calvin to set her plan in motion, she had to offer him an incentive. All she had to do was suck him off real good and he would be following her lead in no time.

## ❧ 17 ❧

Adjusting to motherhood was no joke, but Ryleigh loved every minute of it. Luckily, Zay and his brothers had moved everything into their new home by the time she and Reign were released from the hospital. Zay was a big help and she couldn't ask for a better man. She had to practically fight with him because all he did was hold Reign and had her spoiled rotten. Every time Reign would wake up in the middle of the night for one of her feedings, Zay was always the first to jump up and grab her while Ryleigh rested. Jaylin was also a great little helper and loved having a sister.

"I don't mind coming over and helping out on the cooking tip, but you gon' have to start learning how to cook since you got a family now," Remi told her as she pulled a pan of baked chicken out the oven.

"I know, but what if Zay doesn't like my food?" Ryleigh whispered as she gently patted Reign's back.

"Well, bitch, you gotta start somewhere," Remi replied as she washed her hands. "Here, give her to me so you can make Jaylin's plate. You know I gotta get my time in before Zay comes back hogging her." Remi frowned. When it came to Reign, everybody had to damn near argue with Zay just to hold her, including

Ryleigh. She washed her hands and made Jaylin a plate and sat it on the table.

"Too late for that, he's walking in the door now," Ryleigh announced.

"Hey, baby, that ass looking real fat in them lil' leggings," Zay said as he embraced her in a hug and gripped her round ass.

"Four more weeks, babe," Ryleigh reminded him as she slapped his hands away.

"Aight, but that mouth work though."

"Zay!" Ryleigh squealed as her face turned a bright shade of red.

"You know what, on that note, I'ma head on out." Remi frowned as she kissed Reign on the cheek and placed her in Zay's arms.

"What I do, sis?" Zay laughed as Remi said her goodbyes.

"Hey Daddy!" Jaylin greeted as he came down the large spiral staircase and into the kitchen.

"Sup man, you ready to eat?" Jaylin nodded his head and sat down at the table to eat his food. Ryleigh fixed their plates and they joined him.

Once the kitchen was clean and Jaylin was in bed, Ryleigh went into the master bathroom so that she could take a shower. Her stomach was finally starting to look smaller just like her doctor said it would. At first, Ryleigh didn't think she would be able to breastfeed Reign because she wasn't latching on, but by the time they left the hospital Reign's greedy ass knew exactly what to do.

"Babe, I need to talk to you about something," Ryleigh said as she stepped out the bathroom with a towel wrapped around her body.

"Aw shit. What I do?" Zay joked as he put Reign in her bassinet. Ryleigh had been dreading this day, but she knew something had to be said.

"Nothing like that. I wanted to talk to you about Jasmine. I know the type of man you are and you stand on your children.

There is no easy way to say this, but I think you should have King tested," Ryleigh admitted, sighing heavily. She had been tiptoeing around the issue for a few months. She was happy that she had finally gathered enough courage to say what no one else would. Zay looked at her like she had lost her mind.

"Ryleigh, why the fuck would I have my son tested? What, you don't think he's mine?"

"I don't know, Zay. That's why I think you should have him tested."

"Fuck outta here with the shit, man. If that's the case, then I need to have Reign tested too then." Zay shot back, hurting Ryleigh's feelings.

"Really, Zay? How could you say something like that?"

"Exactly! How the fuck you gon' come at me talkin' 'bout I need to have my son tested? You sound crazy," Zay fumed as he went into their closet and came back out fully dressed.

"Zay, where are you going? Don't leave, I didn't mean anything by it. I just think you should at least consider it," Ryleigh tried to reason.

"Consider what, Ryleigh? You don't think I ain't heard Remi tell you that you need to talk to me about how much money I'm dishing out to my baby mamas? Yeah, I heard that shit. You need to tell Remi to stay out my fucking business. Fuck I look like getting my son tested 'cus yo' ass don't want me paying Jasmine's bills!" Zay barked, grabbing his keys off the dresser.

"Zay I would never—"

"I don't give a fuck about none of that shit you talkin' 'bout, shorty. You on dumb shit and I ain't wit' it."

"So we gon' just ignore the fact that you paying the rent for both of them bitches? Not only that, you still be giving Jasmine money on top of paying her rent, so what, y'all still fuckin' or something?" Ryleigh countered. She understood him being a good dad, but Zay was doing way too much.

"You know what? Fuck this shit, I'm out!" Zay said, walking out of their bedroom, slamming the door behind him.

For the next few days, Ryleigh and Zay still hadn't spoken to one another. Zay still did his normal routine with Reign and Jaylin, but that was about it. He still didn't stay gone for more than a few hours at a time, and if he did, he made sure someone was there to help Ryleigh. In Ryleigh's eyes, the whole argument was stupid and every time she tried to talk to him, he would ignore her.

Zay kissed Reign and grabbed Jaylin's overnight bag so that he could spend the weekend at his grandmother's house. He left without saying anything to Ryleigh and several minutes later, there was a knock on the door. Ryleigh swung the door open and rolled her eyes upward when she saw Isa standing there.

"Well, hey to you too, mean ass," Isa snapped. Ryleigh was lucky she wanted to see Reign or else she would've cursed her out.

"I'm sorry, sister. I'm just having a bad day," Ryleigh revealed as she turned on her heels and walked into the living room.

"Tell me about it. Zane keeps having to go out of town. If that nigga keeps acting like I'm not carrying his child, he gon' be walking down the aisle by his damn self," Isa fussed as she rubbed her small baby bump.

"Don't do my brother like that." Ryleigh laughed. "Girl, remember how I told you that I didn't think King was his?"

"He got him tested?" Isa asked with wide eyes.

"No, but I did mention that he should and he went off on my ass." Ryleigh sighed as she recalled what happened to Isa.

"Maybe you should talk to Zane and Mir about it. They would probably be the ones to get him on board. It might come to blows, but he may look at it differently if it comes from his brothers," Isa suggested.

"You know what? I just might do that," Ryleigh said as she got up to go get a crying Reign. When she came back downstairs, Isa was already standing at the bottom of the staircase with her arms outstretched.

"Give me my baby before Zay comes back," Isa stated. They sat and watched reruns of *Martin* and ordered pizza for the remainder of the evening until they fell asleep.

"Isa, you might as well sleep in one of the guest bedrooms. Zane's flight won't be here until three in the morning," Zay advised, lightly tapping her on the shoulder.

"What time is it?" Isa asked, yawning and stretching her arms out.

"Yeah, you might as well stay so I can have somebody to talk to," Ryleigh snapped, rolling her eyes at Zay.

"I'll just tell Zane to meet me here and we can go home in the morning, because I'm not waking up out of my sleep to go home once he gets here." Isa grabbed Reign and headed upstairs, leaving Zay and Ryleigh alone.

"Zay, this is immature. You can't just walk around here not communicating with me," Ryleigh started. Zay was about to open his mouth to say something but was interrupted by the ringing of the doorbell. When he opened the door, there were two police officers outside.

"Are you Mr. Zaylin Perry?" one of the officers asked.

"Yeah, why, wasup?"

"Mr. Perry, you are under arrest for the murder of Justin White," the officer said as he instructed Zay to place his hands behind his back and read him his Miranda rights.

"Nooooo, what's going on? He's innocent, you can't take him to jail!" Ryleigh screamed.

"Excuse me, ma'am, I'm going to have to ask you to calm down please."

"Fuck you!" Ryleigh spat as Isa came running downstairs upon hearing all the commotion.

"Ryleigh, what happened?"

"They taking my baby to jail!" Ryleigh sobbed as she watched them place Zay in the back of the squad car. Zay mouthed the words, "I love you," and at that moment, Ryleigh lost it. Ryleigh remembered the day Zay confessed to murdering Leah's brother, but never in a million years did she think he would be picked up for it.

Isa ran to comfort Ryleigh, but she was inconsolable. "Ryleigh, calm down, I'm going to call Zane." Isa tried to remain calm for the sake of her sister, but she was panicking inside. All Ryleigh kept repeating was "for murder, for murder." That's when Isa knew it wasn't no petty charge. Jaylin was on the stairs with a confused look. Isa didn't know how much he witnessed, but it was enough to make him cry. She ran to his side, rubbing his back.

"Jaylin, you want to be a big boy for Auntie Isa?" He nodded his head yes with the biggest smile. "Okay, go get you a bag and grab your favorite toys. I'm going to call Uncle Zane to come get us." Ryleigh was in the living room still screaming at the top of her lungs, startling Reign. Isa ran up the stairs, two at a time, grabbing her crying niece. "Lord, please, if I don't ask for anything else, please give me some strength." Reign was nudging towards Isa's boobs, signaling her hunger. Isa bounced Reign up and down, shifting her weight from one leg to the next.

"Auntie, I got everything." Jaylin held up his Paw Patrol bookbag.

"Good boy, baby, c'mon." Isa came back down the stairs. "Ryleigh, I don't care how you do it, but you're going to feed my niece, she's hungry." Isa placed her niece in her mother's arms. Ryleigh zoned out, she was no longer there. Isa could tell, but she propped Reign up on her boob to feed her. Isa turned to search for her cellphone, and after five minutes of looking she located it. Isa dialed Zane's number numerous times with it going straight to voicemail. By the grace of God, she had hoped he landed faster than anticipated, but luck wasn't on her side. Next, she called Remi's number.

"Remi, Zay was arrested, I need you and Mir to haul ass over here, now!" Without much detail, Isa hung up the phone and paced the floor. "Ryleigh, I'm going to get you and Reign packed. Can you be calm while I do that?"

"Isa, I'm not one of them patients you deal with, go ahead, I'm fine." She gave her a reassuring smile. Isa did a double take over her shoulder before she went to pack their bags.

Ten minutes later, Remi and Mir were walking through the front door. "Hey y'all, umm, I'm not sure who y'all lawyers are, so Mir, please call Zay one." Isa hopped up from the sofa so fast, a dizzy spell hit her and she fell back down.

"Aight, sis, you need to sit down, you've done enough," Mir told Isa. Isa wanted to object but she knew he was right, so she sat back down while Remi brought her bottled water.

"So what happened?" Mir asked, looking at the women. Ryleigh ran the story down to Mir. Isa hadn't gotten the full story, so learning that Zay was going down for murder had stunned her. She knew they were in the streets, but she didn't think any of them had caught any bodies. Isa was drained and now questioning Zane. As if on cue, Zane walked through the doors with a worried look on his face. He had seen the numerous missed calls from Isa and texts stating it was an emergency, so his mind was all over.

"Wassup y'all, what's the emergency?" Zane walked over to an exhausted Isa. Mir gave him the head nod for him to follow him. Zane kissed Isa on the lips and followed Mir to the kitchen.

"They talking 'bout murder, yo. I called the lawyer already, but we need to get down to the precinct to find out everything."

"Murder? What the fuck? Since when was Zay out here clipping bodies and shit?" Zane was shocked. "This nigga was being reckless and not keeping us in the loop, fuck!" Zane shouted, starling the women and kids. He was stressed, and learning his brother was going down for murder only made him want to put his ear to the streets. "Yo, we dipping out, y'all go to Remi's house and chill out there until we call y'all."

"Zane, where are you going?" Isa ran to Zane. She was not thinking with her head right now, she was acting on emotion. "Can you be careful?"

"Ma, relax, I'm just going to see about Zay, just trust me and get you and your sisters to the house." The sound of Zane's phone ringing pulled him from his embrace with Isa and he pulled it out his pocket. When Isa saw Casey's name pop up on the screen, she sucked her teeth.

"This bitch," she mumbled.

"Don't start, Isa." Zane answered the call. "Aight Casey, just calm down, I'll be there when I can, fuck."

"What now?" Isa asked Zane.

"This bitch Tayvin off her meds and she kicked Casey and the kids out."

"Casey got a place, they will be fine," Isa told him in a serious tone. Zane waved her off and waved for Mir to follow him out.

"I swear I hate them stupid bitches," was all Isa said before grabbing up the bags so they could go to Remi's house.

## ❧ 18 ❧

"This shit is all for the birds, yo. Zay out here catching bodies and the baby mamas from hell are starting back up." Zane hit the steering wheel as he pulled up to the jail house. "This Biggs better be straight forward too." The lawyer pulled up right behind Zane. They stepped out of the car at the same time. Before going in, they chopped it up with the lawyer, giving him the rundown on everything they knew. Their lawyer stood there taking in everything before he went to go see Zay. Zane and Mir waited for the lawyer to give them the update.

"Mir, can you believe he killed that nigga?"

"Yo, bruh, honestly that shit is crazy." Mir and Zane were back in the car, smoking a blunt.

"The nigga could have had me handle that shit. Something ain't right, though, this got Leah name all over it."

"You think?"

"Nigga, why else would the shit be coming out right now? Think about it, Leah in her feelings like a typical bitch scorned."

"Yea, I feel you on that, but wassup with your baby mamas?"

Zane let a sigh out. "Nigga, I really fucked up getting them two pregnant, fa'real, especially Tayvin." Zane told Mir all that he was dealing with from his baby mamas. When he cut them off, he expected drama, but he didn't expect for them to team up and try to keep him for themselves. "I know I gotta go see Tayvin, 'cus if she acting up she will start harassing Isa, and I can't have that, but I know going to check on her is like setting myself up for the kill."

"What, Isa won't let you go see Tayvin? Not for nothing, bruh, Tay has held you down on more than one occasion, and you don't want her harming Zion like Leah's stupid ass did," Mir told him sternly.

"Nah, you're definitely right, we can't see Zay right now, so I'ma go run by Tay's and check on her."

"No doubt, I'll keep you posted."

Zane opened up his phone to order an Uber. He planned to be in and out of Tayvin's house in thirty minutes. When he showed up, he wasn't expecting to see her sitting at the island with a drink in hand.

"What brings your dirty dick having ass here?"

"Tayvin, c'mon, I thought we were bigger than this." Zane walked up on her and took the glass of Patrón from her hand. She reeked of alcohol, making him turn up her lip at him. Her hair was matted to her head and her clothes looked disheveled. Tayvin had definitely sunk back into a depression. "Help me help you." Tayvin turned to look at him and laughed in his face.

"You want to help me, cute, since when?"

"Tayvin, you think I want you out here fucking up and losing yourself?" Zane knew all too well how to play the game to get her to cooperate. He ran his hand down her face. Tayvin wasn't an ugly girl, but her attitude made her look otherwise. She was smart and handled business when needed but after the breakup, she started losing herself.

"Zane, if you gave a damn about me, I would be carrying your baby, wearing your engagement ring, living in that fucking big ass condo and helping run that restaurant!" Tayvin hopped down from the stool and hit Zane over and over in his chest. Instead of stopping her, he allowed her to get out her anger.

"Tayvin, you know we weren't happy."

"Fuck that! If we weren't happy, why were you here?" she yelled with black mascara running down her face. "You let a child, a fucking teenager, come in and change the way you view life, why her?"

"Tayvin, you don't want me to answer that. C'mon, let me get you cleaned up." Zane pulled Tayvin towards the room. She yanked her arm back and stormed back to the kitchen.

"Have a drink with me, Zane, like old times, just us two," he heard her yell over the running water in the bathroom. Zane thought if it would calm her down, then he was game.

"Tayvin, don't give me a straight drink, mix my shit with juice." Zane went to grab a towel and washcloth. Tayvin entered the bathroom holding two glasses of Patrón mixed with lemonade. "Come get in this tub." Zane wasn't trying to scare her, but he wanted her to listen to him. He took the glasses from her hands. "You're not drinking anymore, you are taking your medicine before I leave."

"When will that be, Zane?" she asked him with a raised brow.

"As soon as you are settled in bed." Tayvin rolled her eyes. She stripped and slid under the warm water. Zane sat on the toilet, taking sips from his drink. He and Tayvin talked and reminisced, and by the time he realized he was finished with his drink, she was stepping out of the tub. Zane got up, staggering a bit before leaning up against the wall.

"Damn, that drink was strong as hell, Tayvin." He patted his pockets looking for his phone. Tayvin watched him with a smirk on her face. Zane pulled his phone from his pocket, dropping it on the floor. He bent down to get it and fell forward on the bathroom floor. Tayvin ran to him, shaking and tapping him. "Yo, call my girl, call my girl."

Tayvin chuckled, she wasn't calling Isa. She used this to her advantage. Tayvin flipped him over on his back. He looked as if he was asleep, but Zane was far gone.

"See, Zane, I tried to ask you nicely, now look at you." Tayvin pulled down Zane's sweats. His semi-erect dick sprang from his boxers. Tayvin licked her lips and took him in her mouth. Zane was moaning in pleasure, turning her on. Tayvin sucked his dick until it was fully erect, and straddling him, she slid down on top of him.

"Hmm," was all Zane could mutter. Tayvin rode Zane until he came, shooting his seeds inside of her.

"Yea, we're gonna see who has the last laugh." Tayvin got up from Zane, wiping her pussy with the washcloth and then Zane. She didn't need him knowing what transpired. All while laughing, she cleaned him up. Tayvin knew her medicine mixed with the Patrón wouldn't hold him over for long. She thought quickly on her feet. Tayvin left and returned with bottled water. "Zane, get up, are you okay?" She put on her best Grammy performance. Zane stirred on the floor. "What? Where?" He closed his eyes tightly, then opened them.

"Oh my god, Zane, thank God you're okay, I was scared."

"Pass me my phone, I gotta go." Zane got up, staggering forward.

"Maybe you need to call someone to get you."

"Nah, I'm good." Zane got outside and stood on the stairs, leaning against the gate. He called Mir to come get him. Something was off, he was drowsy and lost on what caused it.

"Bruh, wassup?"

"Nigga, I need to go home. I'm fucked up, my head pounding, and my stomach ain't right." Zane's body was rejecting the medicine, causing him to break out in a sweat. "Hurry up, something off, yo," was all Zane said before he fell forward down the steps, hitting the ground hard.

"Oh my god, Zane!" was the last thing he remembered hearing. Tayvin went into the house and locked her door. If she acted like she was sleep when he left, she could play off knowing what was going on.

Mir pulled up and almost shit bricks when he saw his brother passed out on the ground. Parking his car, he got out and ran over to Zane and tried to shake him awake. He knew for a fact Tayvin had done something, he just didn't know what. Pulling out his phone, he called Tayvin and didn't get an answer.

"Fuck!" Mir shouted as he slapped Zane's face several times, causing him to grimace in pain. "Zane, wake up, bruh. What happened?" Mir quizzed with a concerned look on his face as he helped Zane stand to his feet.

"Damn, how I get out here?" Zane asked, looking around. Pulling himself together, he leaned on the hood of Mir's car in a feeble attempt to hold himself up. "Yo, I need to lay down for a minute," Zane announced. Mir opened up the passenger side door and helped Zane get in the car.

"All I know is you called me talking 'bout something was off," Mir explained. Then it hit him.

"Yo, I'ma fuck that bitch Tayvin up. I swear to God, I ain't never put my hands on a bitch, but I'ma kill her ass! That bitch drugged me," Zane fumed as he attempted to get out the car.

"Nah, bruh, chill out. We got shit to handle, remember?"

"Yeah, let me go handle this bitch right quick," Zane objected as he opened the car door. With each movement, his head started spinning faster. Mir didn't have to stop Zane from getting out of the car, because he fell back on his own.

Once he realized he was no good, he laid his head back on the headrest and closed his eyes. Tayvin was out of control and he needed to figure out how he was going to handle her without killing her.

"I'm bouta pull up at the crib so you can chill out for a minute," Mir announced, hopping on the highway. Zane's eyes popped open with a quickness.

"Nah, fam, you trippin' like a mufucka. I can't let Isa see me like this!" Zane expressed. He knew for a fact that if Isa found out what happened, she would lose it.

"Fuck you gon' do then, nigga? Either we gon' pull up at Leah's or I'm goin' home."

"I'm straight, pull up at Leah's."

## ⚜ 19 ⚛

It had been a little more than a week since the night of Zay's arrest, and Ryleigh was losing her mind. She and the kids had been staying over Mir and Remi's house, but she was ready to go back home. Jaylin kept asking for his father and at first, Ryleigh didn't know what to tell him. When Remi suggested that she tell him that Zay was away on vacation, she wasted no time sitting Jaylin down and explaining that to him. Hopefully, that would buy some time until Zay could get released on bond.

The only comfort Ryleigh had was knowing that she could at least hear Zay's voice. Since he had been gone, he made sure to call her at least three times a day. That wasn't enough, though. She needed to see and feel her man. She needed Zay to hold her in his arms and tell her that everything was going to be okay and that this was all a bad dream.

Ryleigh had been so deep in thought that she hadn't noticed that Zay's phone was ringing. When she saw Jasmine's name flash across the screen, she wasted no time answering the call. She had been calling him non-stop for the past week, and Ryleigh was sick of it. Enough was enough, Ryleigh decided that it was time to call Jasmine out on her shit.

"Yeah," Ryleigh answered.

"Um, where my baby daddy at?"

"He's currently unavailable. Why, what you need?"

"Tell baby daddy the rent is due. And I need my hair and nails done too," Jasmine shot back.

"Is that right?"

"Bitch, you heard me. Tell that nigga to run me my shit."

"Well, seeing as though you gotta go through me, I ain't got shit for you. You know good and damn well King ain't his baby," Ryleigh snapped.

"Girl, stop playing with me. King is his and he knows that. Don't get cute because he got you living up in that big ass house. Matter fact, he ain't tell you how he was over here fucking on me?" Jasmine spat, pissing Ryleigh off.

"Bitch, please. Zay wouldn't touch you with a ten-foot pole. Anyway, Zay's locked up, so I don't know what to tell you," Ryleigh said, hanging up the phone. She couldn't wait to talk to Zay again. If he was still fucking with Jasmine behind her back, she was done with his ass. Her heart was fragile and Zay was only making it worse. Here she was, sick without him, only for his baby mama to tell her that they were still fucking. Today was Zay's bond hearing and she had to put on her game face while hoping for the best outcome. Ryleigh couldn't allow Zay to see her looking stressed out. The last thing she needed was for Zay to think she couldn't handle things on her own.

"Ryleigh?" Remi repeated.

"Huh?"

"Mir's outside waiting for you," Remi said, interrupting her thoughts. Ryleigh kissed Reign and checked on Jaylin before she got in the car with Mir. The ride to the courthouse was a silent one. Ever since the day she had blasted him out about Dior, their relationship had been strained.

"Mir, I know you probably don't want to hear this but—"

"It's all good, lil' sis. I ain't even mad at you. Honestly, you were doing what any loyal sister would've done, and I can't fault you for that. Even though I meant well, I still should've told

Remi about me working so closely with Dior. Remi's crazy ass won't even let a nigga touch her." Mir laughed, in attempt to lighten the mood.

"I don't even know why she's holding out like that. She'll come around soon, trust me," Ryleigh assured him. Remi was dick crazy, so the fact that she'd gone this long without sex was shocking to Ryleigh. "Mir, can I ask you something? Do you think he's going to get a bond?"

"I don't know, we just gon' hope for the best," Mir replied, turning up the volume on the radio. He was fucked up by the situation, but he would never show it. In Zay's absence, he would just simply step up and handle business like his brother would.

The bond hearing was emotional for Ryleigh. The little hope she did have diminished once the judge announced that he was denying Zay's bond. His next court date was three months from now, and she didn't know how she was going to manage without him around. Once again, Ryleigh felt like her heart had been ripped out of her chest. She didn't understand why Leah couldn't just move on with her life.

"Are you sure you want to go home, Ryleigh?" Remi asked as she helped carry the rest of their bags to the car.

"Yes, Remi, I'm sure. Honestly, I feel so lost right now, but I'm stronger than that. It's not just about me. I love Zay, but I have a daughter who is watching me. I can't ever let her see me fold under pressure, and I won't," Ryleigh affirmed. She was sad, but she'd made up her mind that no matter the outcome, she was going to continue to push forward. She owed it to both Reign and Jaylin. Most importantly, she owed it to herself.

"I can spend the night if you want me to."

"And that's another thing. You and Mir need some privacy. Stop being petty holding out on that man. Remi, Mir loves the fuck out of you, a blind person can see that," Ryleigh said, shocking her sister.

"I know, Ry, he just had me fucked up, so I had to teach him a lesson. But you're right though, because it's only so much Pornhub a bitch can take. I need the real thing." Remi laughed. "Cynthia called me," Remi blurted out. Ryleigh slowly turned her head in Remi's direction. Hearing Cynthia's name made her cringe.

"What did she say?"

"She told me not to ever call her phone again. All I was trying to do was bring our family back together again."

"Why don't you just leave it alone, Remi?" In her opinion, Remi was only making things worse.

"As much as I hate to admit it, Ryleigh, that's still our mother."

"Shut up! Don't you dare say that shit to me. I tried to reach out to her and she never once responded. The day she told me and everybody else that I was a liar and had me sent away was the day she stopped being my mother. Just face it, Remi, that lady will never be a mother to us. Don't you get it? All she ever cared about was Isaac," Ryleigh fumed.

Later that evening, Ryleigh and the kids were all settled back into their home. She ordered pizza for dinner and Jaylin was out for the night. Once she was done feeding Reign, she laid her down in her bassinet so she could take a shower. Usually, she would shower and then cuddle up with Zay and watch a good movie until she fell asleep, the only difference was, Zay wasn't there.

Turning on the shower, Ryleigh checked the temperature of the water and stepped in. She let the hot water massage her back and she could feel the tension slowly start to leave her body. Once she was done, she checked her phone and saw that she had missed a call from Isa. Ryleigh was about to call her back when she heard a noise downstairs.

"Jaylin, is that you?" Ryleigh quizzed as she opened the door to his room. When she realized he was still sleeping, she quietly closed the door and went downstairs to make sure the alarm was set. She was starting to think that maybe she should've stayed over Remi's.

The house was so massive that Ryleigh could hear her own footsteps echoing against the walls. Stopping at the front door, she checked to make sure it was locked before turning on the alarm and heading back upstairs.

"Bitch, I know you didn't think I was gon' just let you take my man and my son!" Leah spat. Ryleigh froze and was forcefully hit over the head, causing her to fall to the ground.

Ryleigh grimaced in pain as she blinked rapidly. She touched the back of her head and panicked when she saw blood. She wasn't sure how long she had been out, but she was certain it was more than a few minutes because she didn't hear any movement. Standing to her feet, Ryleigh ran up the steps two at a time, stopping at Jaylin's room.

"Jaylin?" Ryleigh called out, pulling the comforter back. Tears flooded her eyes as she ran to the opposite end of the hallway.

"Oh my god, no!" Ryleigh screamed in agony. Hands shaking, she frantically searched for her phone. Once she located it, she called the first number she saw.

"Hello?"

"Isa! She's gone!" Ryleigh screamed into the phone.

"Ryleigh, slow down. I can't hear you."

"My baby, she took Jaylin and my fucking baby! He said he would never let anything happen to her, and now she's gone!" Ryleigh sobbed into the phone.

To be continued...

Made in the USA
Monee, IL
15 July 2021